DONALD
and
MELANIA

75 DAYS

OSCAR VALDES

This book is a production of Editorial Madruga,
P.O. Box 78, Pasadena CA 91102
You may visit the author online at oscarvaldes.net

Library of Congress Control Number: 2017953601

Published 2017
Printed in the United States of America
Print ISBN: 978-0-9793558-3-7
E ISBN: 978-0-9793558-4-4

Cover and interior design by delaney-designs.com

For my daughter

PREFACE

July, 30th, 2017

Dear Mr. Trump,

You are in a special position as President of our country and as such have a powerful influence on all our lives. However, at the time of this writing, the nation is deeply divided and you are showing little inclination to bring us together. It is imperative that you start this process.

I am sure that your base is willing to be patient while you find your balance, but find it you must. Seeing you do so will act as a strong impetus for all of us to start a dialogue that is productive and not drenched in animosity.

As in all nations, some Americans have greater ability, some are more industrious, some are kinder than others. But in our hearts and minds, we yearn for a homeland that is united because that is where our strength lies.

Should the present state of disarray in the White House persist, we will be projecting an image of vulnerability that is not in our overall best interest. Furthermore, we cannot retreat from our position of leader of the free world and an example to other nations. It took the blood and efforts of many men and women to get us to this point.

True leadership is not about personal aggrandizement. It is about problem solving and bringing out the best in all of us. More than ever our world needs a champion of democracy. Can you become one?

It is my opinion that your wife can play a decisive role in your finding your path. When we drift into confusion, all of us need the help of someone close who can breathe our anxieties and help us reset.

Not knowing you, your wife, or anyone remotely close to you, I have instead taken an imaginative leap to craft the scenes that follow.

May your term draw us closer, for untold riches await, and America will be greater.

Oscar Valdes
Los Angeles CA

1/20/17 — Inauguration Day. Trump tweets that he is giving power back to the American People. Wealth, jobs, will all be back. America First.

1/22 — Women march in protest, fearing that hard earned gains will be rolled back. Some of the signs read—REFUGEES WELCOME—SCIENCE IS REAL—BLACK LIVES MATTER—FLINT NEEDS CLEAN WATER. Many marchers wear "pussy hats", referring to Trump's grabbing unsuspecting women's genitals.

1/26 — Sally Yates, acting Attorney General (holdover from the Obama administration), calls the White House to inform that General Michael Flynn, National Security Adviser, was "vulnerable to Russian blackmail" (based on business dealings he had had with Russian companies).

1/27 — Trump issues an executive order suspending indefinitely Syrian refugees from entering the U.S. and suspending for 120 days the entrance of citizens from Iraq, Iran, Libya, Sudan, Somalia and Yemen (All the countries listed are predominantly Muslim but none of the 9/11/2001 attackers came from those countries)

Later that day, in a private dinner, Trump tells FBI director Comey, "I need loyalty. I expect loyalty." He wanted Comey to let go of part of the investigation into Mike Flynn.

1/28 — Angela Merkel, the German chancellor, explains to Trump the Geneva convention, which requires nations to protect war refugees.

1/29 — As protests to the executive order suspending entry to the U.S. mount across the land,

Mr. Trump stated, "This is not a Muslim ban, as the media is falsely reporting. This is not about religion, this is about terror and keeping our country safe."

1

They are lying in bed in their ample bedroom in the White House. There is a bathroom across from the bed and next to its entrance is a round table with two chairs. Donald is eating from a bag of chips.

Melania — But why?

Donald — Because it's easier. Because people are busy with their lives and if you break it down for them, then they'll remember it. America First! Now that's a heck of a slogan, isn't it? Can't go wrong with that. And I said to them, 'Muslims are a threat to us. Solution, stop them from coming in'. And I said, 'Illegal Mexicans are rapists. Solution, build the wall'. And I said, 'Put her in jail'. Crowds loved that one, didn't they? It was not polite conversation but I'm already 70 years old and wanted to get to the White House. If I had tried to be nice to all those bozos I had to debate, we wouldn't be here now, sharing this beautiful bedroom full of history.

Melania — You make it sound very simple...

Donald — There was a trick to it, mind you, and it was finding the right audience. That's where my genius came in.

Melania — Do you really believe what you said to them?

Donald — Of course I do. That's why I was so convincing. I can make anything sound convincing.

Melania — Never mind standards of decency...

Donald — I was getting people excited, wasn't I? They'd never seen someone like me on the stump. People heard there was a show in town and they came to see it and they got one. They went home feeling refreshed, lighter, happier. And they told their neighbors...

Melania — And the excitement spread...

Donald — And I said, there's nothing wrong with you. Look, it's those over there, the ones with the funny accents and that other religion, those are the heathen, those are the cause of your grief. Behold the liberals and their decadent values, the abortion righters, the immigrant lovers! They are in cahoots with those who are stealing what rightfully belongs to you. (he smiles proudly) And it helped very much, of course, that I didn't need a job, that I swooped into town in my own jet with TRUMP painted across, that I look like a Viking, that I am *the greatest* real estate mogul New York has ever seen, that I have oodles of money and was flying in to bring them the freedom they had lost. In other words, I was the angel they had been waiting for.

He turns to her and offers his bag of chips.

Melania — No, thanks.
Donald — C'mon, it's not going to kill you.
Melania — I said no.
Donald — I hate it that you have that self control.
Melania — Just say no, it's not that hard.
Donald — As accomplished as I am, when it comes to junk food, I just lose it.
Melania — I have to worry about my figure.
Donald — But now that you're the first lady...
Melania — The more reason to do so. I have a responsibility to the nation.

He eats a couple more chips.

Donald — Isn't that something, first time I run for office, any office, and I become president of this country. How many people can say that? I think I'm the first.
Melania — I think other people have done it.
Donald — I'll ask Reince to research it for me.
Melania — I'll do it. Reince has more important things to do.
Donald — It's important to me, okay. I'll ask Reince. Or one of my generals.

He offers her the bag of chips again.

Melania — No is no. N—O.

Donald — Suit yourself. (laughs to himself) Don't you like the sound of it?

Melania — What?

Donald — One of *my* generals.

Melania — Don't be fooled. They have their own minds.

Donald — Can't you just go along with me for a minute? When I was in real estate I had lieutenants, now I have generals. Love it.

Melania — Dee, about the travel ban...

Donald — It's not a ban. I like being first... ever since I was a kid. In fact, I did a lot of things just to be first. Sometimes naughty things.

Melania — Like what?

Donald — I was the first in my class to put a thumbtack in the teacher's seat. Boy, he jumped fast out of that one. We didn't have recess for the rest of the day.

Melania — The other kids loved you for it.

Donald — I know. Sometimes I don't think of the consequences.

Melania — Dee, the travel restriction...

Donald — You know what I should get and I'm not hearing any rumors about it?

Melania — What?

Donald — A Nobel prize.

Melania — You're not serious?

Donald — Why not?

Melania — You haven't done anything.

Donald — Obama hadn't either and he got it?

Melania — That was different.

Donald — How so?

Melania — He was the first African American elected to the office and his message was one of hope and inclusion. He wanted to reach out to everybody. Didn't you read his book? I put it on your desk.

Donald — I was busy. Anyhow, you gave me the gist of it.

Melania — You have to read it.

Donald — Listen to me. I deserve the Nobel Prize because I want to unite this country.

Melania — Unite?

Donald — Yes. Listen for a minute. That's a problem you have, you know that? You don't listen.

She throws up her hands in exasperation.

Donald — I won the election, darling...
Melania — Don't call me darling.
Donald — Why not?
Melania — I just don't like it.
Donald — Sorry. I won the election because I became the champion of white people who had been forgotten. I, Donald J Trump, will restore what they have lost... pride, status, money, whatever... and then the country will have new energy and we will be great again. When we are great again, we will lead the entire world to happiness and prosperity.
Melania — The white man as savior... the engine of prosperity.
Donald — Nice. I could use that. So my message is not only a message of hope and inclusion but on a much grander scale than Obama's. And that's why I should get the Nobel. And not only one but two.
Melania –Two?
Donald — One for each term.
Melania — Go tell it to the Muslims! And everybody else whose travel you've banned.
Donald — Why are you getting so upset?
Melania — Because it doesn't make any sense.
Donald — Your relatives from Slovenia can still come in.
Melania — I don't care if they come in or not. I'm talking about your message of division, not inclusion. I'm talking about your inciting hate when you go off on your tirades.
Donald — Tirades? Those tirades have got me where I am, so chill out. In fact, you wouldn't be in this bed with the President of the United States if it hadn't been for those tirades of mine. So again, chill out. And enjoy.

She is fuming but says nothing for a moment. He reaches over to caress her but she jumps out of bed, strides to the bathroom and slams the door behind her.

Donald — C'mon, honey. Don't be like that.

A moment passes with no reply.

Donald — (firmly) I'm going to get up, go to the Oval office and write an executive order for you to exit that bathroom immediately. Do I make myself clear? If you don't come out you will be in violation of the laws of this land. Do you read me, Melania? I'm not joking anymore. I am your Commander in Chief. Open the door now!

Silence for a moment. He then gets up and goes to stand by the bathroom door.

Donald — (softening) I know you have some distant relatives that are Muslim, but I promise they will not be affected by the ban... restriction.

The toilet flushes.

Donald — Melania, baby, don't do this to me.

The toilet flushes again.

Donald — Honey... you know how I like to clown around sometimes... but I'm really crazy for you. And please forgive me for not waiting for you when I got out the SUV and stepped up to shake hands with Obama and Michelle on inauguration day, and left you behind with the beautiful present you had got for her. Which Michelle didn't know what to do with. I'm really sorry. I was just a little anxious. Darling... sorry, I mean, cutie pie... you know I can't live without you. C'mon, open up. Honey, I really want some cuchi cuchi time with you... please?

He paces off for a moment, then returns.

Donald — And I'm sorry too for all that nasty talk about girls. I know that in your heart you've forgiven me already, but I wanted to ask anyway.

Then the bathroom door cracks open and Melania sticks her head out to look at him. He smiles. She steps out heading straight back to the bed but he stops her and embraces her.

Donald — I love you so much.

Still peeved, she pulls away and continues to the bed and lies down. He follows and sits by her side. He takes her hand in his.

Donald — (while caressing her hand) Baby, you know me better than anybody else... and you know that, deep down... what I really am is a showman. That's the true Donald. And I tell you, I am still amazed how I managed to land this gig. You have to admit, it was an unbelievable performance. Momentous and historical.
Melania — (warming) It was quite a show.
Donald — Now, I don't really care that much about the Nobel... I'm like... take it or leave it... and the reason is... if I were to get the Nobel for Peace, it might make me gun shy... which is what happened to Obama. See, if he hadn't got that prize, he would've gone into Syria when they used chemical weapons. Getting the Nobel, held him back.
Melania — Lots of innocent people get killed with all those bombings, so I disagree.
Donald — That's okay. You can have your opinion, too.
Melania — Thank you.
Donald — And if Obama hadn't been gun shy, Putin might not have dared to invade the Ukraine. Anyways... what would really mean a lot to me is...

Kissing her hand, lingering as he does, placing it against his face.

Melania — What?

Donald — I shouldn't say...

Melania — Say it.

Donald — I shouldn't, it sounds conceited.

Melania — But that's you, so out with it.

Donald — Okay, then... what would really mean a lot to me is... if I got an Oscar for my electoral performance.

She laughs. He smiles. Then she pulls him to her, they kiss, and she turns the lights off.

1/31/17 — Trump fires Sally Yates, Acting Attorney General, for "refusing to enforce a legal order designed to protect the citizens of the United States."

2/2 — Trump proposes the repeal of the Johnson amendment (after Lyndon Johnson), which would allow churches to endorse politicians. "Pastors should be held accountable to God alone for what they say behind the pulpit, not the IRS."

2/3 — Judge Robart of the Federal District Court in Seattle, temporarily enjoins and restrains government agents from enforcing Trump's travel suspension.

2/5 — Trump tweets—Just cannot believe a judge would put our country in such peril. If something happens blame him and court system. People pouring in. Bad people!

2/7 — Trump tweets—I don't know Putin, have no deals in Russia, and the haters are going crazy—yet Obama can make a deal with Iran, # 1 in terror, no problem!

Trump has yet to reveal his tax returns. The first president not to do so since 1976.

2

Melania is sitting up in bed reading Freud's The Interpretation of Dreams. Donald is sitting at the table, looking at his phone, reading the news and replies to his tweets.

Donald — You're fired! That's the way it's going to be. Period.

Melania — She was standing up for what she believed.

Donald — And I was, too.

Melania — Were you, really?

Donald — Absolutely. Defending our borders, no matter what. And if I push through the repeal of the Johnson amendment, why all those pastors will be endorsing me next time around. Returning power to the people, that's what I'm all about. Nifty idea, don't you think?

Melania — I believe in the separation of church and state.

Donald — Why?

Melania — It helps people think.

Donald — People need guidance...

Melania — Let others think for you and we invite tyranny.

Donald — (smiling) We look to experts, don't we? In health, in technology, in the arts, and we defer to them. Nothing wrong with that. Should be the same with politics.

Melania — Since when have you been an expert in politics?

Donald — (winking at her) Since I called myself one.

She smiles, shakes her head.

Donald — Don't you think I project power?

Melania — No.

Donald — What? How could that be? I just got elected to the most important job in the world.

Melania — You have power but you don't project it.

Donald — First time I hear that. You're serious?

Melania — Why shouldn't I be serious?
Donald — I love your directness.
Melania — No, you don't.
Donald — Are you in a mood today?
Melania — Don't go there.

He puts the phone down, sits back in his chair, pensive, nods to himself.

Donald — I just know Obama tapped my phone. I don't care what anybody says. And you know what? I might just tap his. Tit for tat. What do you think?
Melania — You have a brain but you don't always use it.
Donald — You just don't know politics. My style is to always be on the move, call me mercurial if you'd like.

She puts the book down.

Donald — Does Putin project power?
Melania — A certain kind of power.
Donald — What kind?
Melania — The kind to keep people in line, doing what he wants them to do.
Donald — That's not a bad power to have. What power doesn't he project?
Melania — The power to lift people, to help them better themselves.
Donald — Interesting. Who does that?
Melania — Angela Merkel.
Donald — Hmm. I'm listening.
Melania — It's a soft kind of power but very effective. She makes you want to be like her.

Donald — But that's predictable. You would've chosen a woman. I'm surprised you didn't vote for Hillary.

She gives a sly smile.

Donald — What? You didn't?

Melania — Of course not.

Donald — We'll never know, won't we?

He leans forward in his chair, arms on his knees and stares at her. There's something different about her.

Melania — What are you going to do about Russia's hacking during the election?

Donald — It didn't influence the election.

Melania — Maybe it did and maybe it didn't, but the point is that it happened.

Donald — Don't believe everything the press says.

Melania — They're reporting what the intelligence community is saying. They're experts, aren't they?

Donald — Fake news.

Melania — I find it worrisome that you're giving Russia a free pass. Obama imposed sanctions because they hacked our systems.

Donald — Mike Flynn is a good guy, okay? He's a good guy. The FBI should leave him alone.

Melania — I'm talking about the hacking, not Flynn. Or are they related?

Donald — I didn't need any help from the Russians or anyone else, I won fair and square.

Melania — Did you fire Sally Yates because of her position on the travel ban or because she told you that Mike was "vulnerable to Russian blackmail?"

Donald — What's this, an interrogation?

Melania — I'm your wife. You shouldn't keep secrets from me.

He pauses. Then...

Donald — Melania... I'm President now, and some things I will not share with you.

Melania — Why not?

Donald — Matters of state.

Melania — But you will share them with your confidants?

Donald — They're sworn to secrecy.

Melania — Then go ahead and swear me in.

Donald — Look, you're my wife and everything but...

Melania — You're free to take or not take my opinion but I should be your number one confidante.

Donald — Sweetheart, you do not understand politics.

Melania — I'm learning fast.

Donald — We'll see.

He rubs his face, looks at her in silence.

Donald — So you don't think people want to be like me?

Melania — They may want to have the things you have, but be like you, I don't think so.

Donald — Why not?

Melania — You're too impulsive.

Donald — There's a certain charm that comes with it. Too bad you can't see it.

Melania — I see it, all right, and it worked for you in real estate, but it's a detriment to a sitting President.

Donald — Why are you saying these things to me?

Melania — So you can fix them.

Donald — Why didn't you say them before?

Melania — I was under your spell.

He smiles.

Donald — I'd like for you to fall right back under it.

Melania — Why don't you try something different?

Donald — Romance you all over again?

Melania — Why not? I never said I wanted it to end.

Donald — You really think I can fix these things?

Melania — Yes.

Donald — How?

Melania — Stop tweeting for starters. You're addicted to it.

Donald — And let people get away with what they're saying?

Melania — You don't have to answer everything said about you.

He runs his fingers through his hair, sits back, folding his arms as he looks up at the ceiling.

Donald — I'll consider it.
Melania — Try it for a week.
Donald — It'll make the news, for sure. Real news too.

He glances at the phone. He's itching to get back to it. She watches him.

Melania — It's hard isn't it?

He shrugs.

Melania — And you need to start exercising.
Donald — Golf doesn't count?
Melania — You ride the cart for the long stretches. I've seen you.
Donald — That's going to change. You're always on me about the weight thing. It's not like I don't notice. All of you in the family are lean. The boys, Ivanka, everybody. I'm the only fat one.
Melania — I don't want you to have a heart attack.
Donald — Do you have to say that?
Melania — You're seventy years old, you're under a lot of stress and you're overweight. I'd rather be blunt than sorry.
Donald — Okay, you've said it, I don't want you to keep repeating it.
Melania — I want you to live till you're a hundred.

He sneaks a peek at the phone.

Melania — Can't resist, can you?

He pulls back.

Donald — What do you think I'll gain from not tweeting?
Melania — Poise.

Donald — What? Of all things… poise?

Melania — Yes.

Donald — So I lack poise?

Melania — It comes and goes. And your thinking will improve, too. It won't hurt, for sure.

Donald — Honey… do you love me?

Melania — Very much so. I wouldn't be here if I didn't.

Donald — I don't know sometimes.

He stands and steps over to the window. He looks out. Then turns back to face her.

Donald — Weren't you attracted to me because of my power?

Melania — I was attracted to the thirst you had for it.

Donald — And that was enough for you?

Melania — Yes. It didn't matter that you accomplished all you wanted. What was important was that you had the thirst and worked for it… that you had the passion.

Donald — So even if I didn't reach my goals, you would've been content?

Melania — Yes.

Donald — Even if I hadn't become the most powerful real estate mogul ever?

Melania — Yes.

She puts her book on the night stand, gets up and walks over to the window to join him.

Melania — There's a side to your thirst for power that concerns me.

Donald — What?

Melania — That you're willing to condone wrong doing.

Donald — If you're talking about the Russian hacking…

Melania — I'm talking about your scapegoating Muslims and Mexicans to suit your aims.

Donald — Why didn't you say something when I was doing it?

Melania — I was in denial. (she pauses) It says something about me, doesn't it? I'll have to deal with that.

Donald — You didn't think I'd get elected?

Melania — I didn't. But you were and I've come to realize how the impact of your judgment is far reaching.

Donald — Is it because I've said I like Putin?

Melania — You've gone back and forth on him... but you're approving of el-Sisi in Egypt, the Saudis, Duterte in the Philippines...

Donald — Strong men solving real problems.

Melania — Strong men you call them? To me, they're weak, selfish, cruel, their rigidities a misunderstanding of what masculinity is.

Donald — They are leaders in faraway countries, if that's any consolation.

Melania — There are no faraway countries anymore.

Donald — What's your worry? You think I'll become like them?

Melania — I do.

Donald — Relax. Our system won't let me. We have an independent judiciary that's put a hold on my travel restrictions. And I can't discipline the press the way Xi does in China, or Putin. Look how they make fun of me every day. Do I like it? No. Who would? So, are my instincts autocratic? Yes. Would I like to rule without opposition? Yes. Would I like to get reelected for a second and third term? Yes. And I doubt a political leader was being honest if he said he enjoyed having an opposition.

Melania — Democracy takes effort. True leaders welcome the opposition because they know they are fallible. They welcome it because they know their voice is not the only voice. They welcome it because they recognize the value of being open to scrutiny.

Donald — And maybe they just didn't have the cunning and willpower to prevail.

He walks back into the room and sits at the table.

Donald — I don't think it's good for us to talk politics so much... if you don't mind.

Melania — It cuts to the bone, doesn't it?

Donald — Yes.

Melania — But it doesn't have to be unfriendly…
Donald — (reaching out to her) Come, sit with me.

She goes to him and sits on his lap. They look at each other for a moment.

Donald — This is new territory for both… and it might bring out aspects of mine that are unfamiliar to you… and even to me… I just hope they won't drive us apart.
Melania — We would have to be very honest…

He nods.

Donald — That book you've been reading? (with a hint of disdain) You're getting something out of it?
Melania — It's slow go… but yes, I am.
Donald — I've never been a fan. Will you tell me about it sometime?
Melania — I will.

She rests her head on his shoulder.

7/26/16 — During the campaign, Trump states on television—"Russia, if you're listening, I hope you're able to find the 30,000 emails (from Hillary Clinton) that are missing. I think you will probably be rewarded mightily by our press."

2/13/17 — General Flynn in his letter of resignation as National Security Advisor—"I inadvertently briefed the vice president elect and others with incomplete information regarding my phone calls with the Russian ambassador." The general had discussed the possibility of lifting sanctions imposed by Obama in response to Russian meddling in the presidential election.

2/15 — Trump tweets—The Russian connection nonsense is merely an attempt to cover up the many mistakes made in Hillary Clinton's losing campaign.

2/15 — Trump tweets—Information is being illegally given to the failing @nytimes and @washingtonpost (NSA and FBI?) by the intelligence community. Just like Russia.

2/16 — Trump tweets—Crimea was TAKEN by Russia during the Obama administration. Was Obama too soft on Russia?

2/16 — He tweets—'Trump signs bill undoing Obama coal mining rule' (the stream protection rule was intended to protect waterways from mining waste)

1/22/17 — Trump states—"The only one that cares about my tax returns are the reporters, okay?"

3

He is sitting by the table, eyes glued to the screen of his phone. Melania stands by the window looking out.

Donald — My base expects it from me. They like that instant gratification, the grit that I convey, the snap back, the 'I'm not taking it anymore!' Remember Network, Peter Finch? You're too young to remember.

Melania — I saw it.

Donald — Loved that flick. Finch got the first posthumous Oscar. But back to my base. I'm their champion. They got me elected and by God I'm going to stay true to them. And with the same savvy I built me an empire, I will restore what they've lost. The poor will no longer be poor and the well-off will be even better off. I'm the disrupter, the one who's coming in to change the way we do things.

She turns to look at him.

Melania — You're getting along with your generals?

Donald — I am, indeed. Fine people, too. I'm being criticized for appointing too many to the cabinet but we live in uncertain times and I need their expertise. We have to fight ISIS. Flynn knew a lot about that. I liked him. Too bad he had to resign.

Melania — Good thing he did.

Donald — What?

Melania — Like Sally Yates said, his dealings with Russian companies made him vulnerable to blackmail. Better safe than sorry.

Donald — He's a good guy.

She returns to gazing out the window.

Melania — I read in the newspaper that back in July last year, you openly called for Russia to hack Clinton's emails.
Donald — Ha! Disinformation. What I said was, "I hope you're able to find the emails that are missing". I wasn't asking them to hack anything.
Melania — How else would they find anything except by hacking?
Donald — Look, I misspoke. I take it back. The press put a spin on it. Anyway... if it bothers you so much, why did you wait so long to bring it up?
Melania — I told you, I was in denial. But you'll admit that your loose tongue can hurt you.

He puts the phone down, sits back, folds his arms.

Melania — Is there anything to the Russia investigation?
Donald — Nothing. They can investigate all they want but they will find nothing. But liberals will keep banging on that drum because they still can't get over the fact that I stole the election from right under their noses. They didn't pay attention to those communities in need and how white males had been injured.
Melania — Neither did the republicans before them.
Donald — It's what happened during the Obama years that counts. Democrats were distracted by all the congratulating themselves on the fact that Saint Barrack had descended on earth, and that his amazing grace signaled that race relations had leapt forward and what a historic achievement that was.
Melania — And you saw that there was plenty of room to manipulate the race issue to your advantage.
Donald — Why not, everybody does it.
Melania — No regrets?
Donald — None. I knew it was right there under the surface, I just needed to play it the right way, with the right group.
Melania — You're not concerned you have unleashed forces you may not be able to control?

Donald — The economy will soothe the anger. The markets have been rising since I came aboard. I just need to keep coming up with new ideas... and so long as I keep people entertained...

She walks from the window to join him at the table.

Donald — My main priorities should be very clear to all: put more money in every American's pocket and make us stronger. It's not that complicated.

Melania — You don't think people would mind you becoming an autocrat even if you were to put more money in their pockets?

Donald — Not really. But, as I said before, our system of checks and balances will keep me from usurping power.

Melania — What about your taxes?

Donald — No need to disturb that.

Melania — I'm amazed at how people are not complaining more vigorously. It's such a central issue.

Donald — Why?

Melania — It would give people a clear picture of how successful you really were in real estate.

Donald — Let them look at my hotels, or better, come stay in them.

Melania — You're hiding the truth.

Donald — I disagree.

Melania — Well, then, I'd like to see your tax returns myself.

Donald — (pausing) You haven't asked to see them in the thirteen years we've been married.

Melania — The time has come.

Donald — I'll think about it.

Melania — What's there to think about? I'm your wife and I want to see the returns.

Donald — What's the urgency?

Melania — I'm coming into my own and I want to know where I stand. That should be enough.

Donald — Are you thinking of leaving?

Melania — No, I'm not.

Donald — Okay, I'll talk to my accountant.
Melania — Thank you.

Pause.

Melania — Are you afraid that if the public sees the returns they won't see you as the greatest real estate mogul there ever was?
Donald — I am the greatest, no matter what the records show.
Melania — Then why not make them public?
Donald — I will, eventually. But first I need to consolidate my position.
Melania — You have to keep the fiction going a while longer?
Donald — I like the way you put that.
Melania — A tactical move?
Donald — Exactly.
Melania — For how long?
Donald — As long as I need to. What's the rush, anyway?
Melania — I see a parallel between your relationship with the public and your relationship with me.
Donald — They're two different things.
Melania — No, they're not. If you can't have the truth with the people, then you won't have the truth with me. And if that's the case then we'll end up growing apart.
(she looks him in the eye)
I would prefer that wouldn't happen.
Donald — Neither would I.

She reaches over, extending her hand to him. He takes it and holds it.

Melania — I take responsibility for not being more vocal from the start. If I had been more politically aware... if I had been more open in expressing my opinions... more willing to engage in a political dialogue with you... I may have influenced your positions... and contributed to your political maturation. In one way or another I settled for being the pretty wife... the mother of your son... the nurturer when you needed it... but backed off from being your intellectual partner. That's on me. I take responsibility for that.

Donald — Maybe we wouldn't have been together if you had.

Melania — I now think it's an obligation every woman has to her partner... and every man to his. If not, then the foundation will crack under pressure.

Donald — Is our foundation cracking?

Melania — (pauses briefly) I think it is. Not that we haven't been putting on a good show for the public.

Donald — You think the Obamas had a good partnership?

Melania — I think so. And I'm sure she was her number one confidante.

They look at each other and smile.

Donald — Even if he didn't swear her in.

Melania — Yes.

Donald — And the Clinton's?

Melania — I'm sure they did, too... for the most part.

He nods pensively.

Donald — Don't you miss taking a stroll in Central Park?

Melania — I do.

Donald — What else do you miss?

Melania — Seeing you wearing your hard hat when you went on site to see how construction was going.

Donald — Do you want that back?

She smiles ruefully.

Donald — What do you miss?

Melania — Walking down Fifth Avenue, seeing all the stores... us getting away and going to see a movie in the middle of the day, when there weren't that many people in the theatre.

Donald — Standing in line to buy popcorn...

Melania — Taking our shoes off...

Donald — Remember that time the movie house was nearly empty and we made out sitting in the back row?
Melania — Of course I remember.
Donald — We did that in Paris once, also. That little theatre near the Sorbonne.
Melania — Are those times gone forever?
Donald — I don't know. But you're making me all sad.
Melania — What's our favorite movie?
Donald — (singing softy) Love is a many splendored thing...
Melania — How many times did we see it?
Donald — Oh, so many times, I couldn't say.
Melania — We've seen it 52 times.
Donald — You've kept count?
Melania — I have.

He gives her a long, amorous look.

Donald — Would you like to dance, my dear?
Melania — I would.

They rise and step to the center of the room.

Melania — Wait, I have it here in my cell phone.

She goes back to the table, finds the song and presses play. She returns to his embrace as the music fills the air. (Song by Sammy Fain and Paul Francis Webster)

Donald — Just pretend I'm William Holden.
Melania — Don't be silly. I'm happy to be in your arms.

He leads her in dance to the window where they sway under the moonlit sky.

... Love is a many splendored thing...

2/17/17 – Trump tweets–Despite the long delays by the Democrats in finally approving Dr. Tom Price, the repeal and replacement of Obamacare is moving fast!

Pew Research Center poll – As Republicans in Congress speak of repealing and replacing Obamacare, a poll of 1500 Americans showed that 54% approved of the law passed in 2010 while 43% disapproved -

2/17 – Trump tweets–Going to Charleston, South Carolina, in order to spend time with Boeing and talk jobs! Look forward to it.

2/17 – He tweets–Thank you for all of the nice statements on the Press Conference yesterday. Rush Limbaugh said one of the greatest ever. Fake media not happy!

2/17 – He tweets–Looking forward to Florida rally tomorrow. Big crowd expected!

2/18 – He tweets–The FAKE NEWS media (failing @nytimes, @NBCNews, @ABC, @CBS,@CNN, is not my enemy, it is the enemy of the American People!

2/18 – He tweets–Don't believe the main stream (fake news) media. The White House is running VERY WELL. I inherited a mess and am in the process of fixing it.

2/20 – He tweets–Give the public a break–The FAKE NEWS media is trying to say that large scale immigration in Sweden is working out just beautifully. NOT!

2/21 — He tweets—'Americans overwhelmingly oppose sanctuary cities'

2/23 — He tweets—Seven people shot and killed yesterday in Chicago. What is going on there—totally out of control. Chicago needs help!

2/23 — Gallup Daily: Trump Job Approval (one month after becoming president) 43% approve while 52% disapprove (based on phone interviews with 1500 national adults)

On 2/21/2009, (one month after becoming president) 63% approved of Obama, while 24% disapproved.

4

They're both sitting at the table in their bedroom. They're sipping a rare brand of apple cider.

Donald — Is there any doubt in your mind that my victory was the result of a brilliant strategy?

Melania — In part.

Donald — In part? Honey, I assure you, it will go down as such in the political history of our country. Academics will write books on my success. The man who saved the republican party. After that glorious season of debates when I made every contender—all senators and governors—look like amateurs. Nobody had the guts to come out and challenge me. They all did this little dance thinking that I would go away, that I didn't have the stamina for the long haul, that I was a joke. It was a foregone conclusion that I would lose and so Hillary and her lackeys fell asleep, and in their smugness, even called my people 'deplorable'. And the pollsters—the oracles of the establishment—got drunk celebrating their grand ability to forecast the future. And then Donald roared and with one mighty swing knocked them off their pedestal, and rubbed their faces in the muck. They still can't get over it.

Melania — You do deserve a great deal of credit.

Donald — Thank you. It's good to hear you say that. I wouldn't mind hearing it more often.

Melania — Of course.

Donald — I can confidently say that the party owes me—big time- which is why they should be bending over backwards to accommodate me. I have a base, they don't. I am graciously loaning them my base. They have food on the table because of yours truly.

Melania — Let's toast to that.

She raises her glass and he follows. They clink and sip.

Donald — Very good. Great aroma. Subtle bouquet. I've always been fond of high living.

Melania — You've worked for it.

Donald — Thank you.

Melania — You identified people in need...

Donald — I have always felt a deep connection to my brothers and sisters...

Melania — Always?

He stares at her.

Melania — But you certainly took them by surprise... the blustery style, the actor in you.

Donald — (smiling appreciatively) Not that Hollywood recognizes it. But thank you, dear. I love hearing you acknowledge my qualities. Here's to that. (raising his glass) Cheers.

They touch their glasses.

Melania — Underneath it all, there was another, even more important factor, that handed you the victory.

Donald — What other factor?

Melania — Women.

Donald — (suspiciously) Women?

Melania — Yes.

Donald — Sorry, it was men—white men. There's consensus on that.

Melania — There are more women than men in this country. And they won you the election by—once again—deferring to men.

Donald — This is going to be interesting. What political analyst are you following these days?

Melania — None. This is my own thinking.

Donald — Your own?

Melania — You don't think I'm capable?

Donald — I didn't say that.

Melania — Here was the second opportunity in history to make a woman President and we blew it. We simply could not find it in ourselves to recognize that we deserve to have a woman leader of all Americans. We could not come to grips with the fact that we had the power—in our hands—to elevate someone who looked like us, who was made like us, who had shared our struggles, to the Oval Office.

Donald — Dear, it's not just about gender... there's more to it.

Melania — It *is* about gender... and color of the skin.

Donald — How can I get through to you...

Melania — The British gave us Thatcher, the Germans gave us Merkel, the Chileans gave us Bachelet, the people from Myanmar gave us Suu Kyi, but we could not find it in ourselves to elect one of our kind.

Donald — But why is it so important?

Melania — Because it will free up something in us, something that we've held back for ages. Identifying with someone like us who is acting on the world stage with confidence, will give us one more handle with which to pull ourselves up and defer to no one on the basis of sex. It will help us further define our relationship with your gender... in the home and in the workplace... and we will no longer be reticent to assert our difference and give free rein to our creativity.

Donald — But Hillary?

Melania — Yes.

Donald — You did vote for her, then?

She stares back.

Donald — I know you did.

Melania — We have internalized the sense that we must defer to men. It's a psychological ball and chain that we carry. A woman President would do wonders for our nation. Look at what Obama did for blacks.

Donald — What did he do? I don't see the difference. Other than leaving me with a mess that I now have to clean up.

Melania — Are you blind? Do you not see the confidence in blacks — both women and men?

Donald — Ben Carson was pretty confident, and way before Obama.

Melania — I see it... white people see it... and it was a factor in your electoral victory.

Donald — Wait a minute, what about my brilliant strategy, that doesn't count anymore?

Melania — On second thought, there was nothing brilliant about it.

She sits back and rests her hands in her lap. Donald looks at her.

Donald — I don't know what it is... but ever since you set foot in the White House you've been on a tear.

Melania — The women... they saw the anguish in their spouses... and they sacrificed once again.

Donald — You're way over your head in making these generalizations. You just spout the stuff, make it up as you go. But no. There has to be scientific rigor to conclusions about complex issues. Melania, dear, I can get someone in the National Institute of Health to do a study. In fact, I'll call the Secretary of Health right now...

Melania — Since when have you waited for scientific rigor to back your allegations?

Donald — That's different. I'm a politician. I can't wait for these things... I have to fly with my thoughts.

Melania — Yes... and women should fly too.

He leans forward in his chair, the mood troubled.

Donald — Look...you've got to slow down a little. When I get home after a busy day... I need some R & R... not a speech on feminism.

Melania — I'm sorry. (gently) Did you want your slippers?

Donald — (surprised) Why, yes, that would be nice.

She gets up, goes to his closet and gets him his slippers. As she kneels before him he reaches out to caress her hair.

Donald — You look beautiful.
Melania — Thank you.
Donald — Come, sit on my lap.

She slides onto him. He caresses her face.

Donald — (softly) See... I know that talking about these issues is important to you... but it doesn't relax me... this here relaxes me...
Melania — It relaxes me, too... the thing is... there's been an imbalance in our life... too much of one and too little of the other...
Donald — Okay... but we can't rush it... the job is overwhelming at times... and there's been a lot of confusion... I have a lot of people running around... with different opinions... different agendas... and I've said and done a lot of things already... but I've yet to feel that I'm in charge... really in charge.

She caresses him.

Melania — We just didn't prepare, did we?
Donald — I suppose we didn't.
Melania — You didn't expect to win...
Donald — True. I thought I should put on a good show anyway—good advertising for my brand—then go back home to my hotels.

She smiles.

Donald — Did you watch me when I was on The Apprentice?
Melania — Didn't miss one.
(she caresses his eyebrows)
Dee... we can always go back to that. I mean... the fact that you got the job doesn't mean that it's right for you.
Donald — You were satisfied with who I was?
Melania — I was... but I also had the sense that we could become better people... and I wasn't doing that. This White House experience has given us a jolt... which is great... but I don't think your running for President has brought out the best in you. We

used to be friends with the Clintons... I liked them... and then you said all those things... so maybe we don't need this.

Donald — I was a bit harsh... I admit it.

Melania — I didn't stand up to you, either.

Donald — You're standing up now.

Melania — I am.

Donald — And we're here.

Melania — It doesn't mean we can't revise the strategy.

Donald — What were you thinking?

Melania — You could focus on doing the one term...

Donald — Just the one term?

Melania — That's enough. And think of enjoying your life... our life. We have enough, Dee... we don't need all of it. Concentrate on what you're really good... and have fun.

Donald — They'll see me as a failure.

Melania — You've already made history. And we could expand the Trump Foundation to help others... like the people who helped elect you. You could do a good term if you really focused on leaving a legacy... something you would be proud of.

Donald — I don't know.

Melania — Think about it.

Donald — You did watch all the episodes of The Apprentice?

Melania — I did.

Donald — I was good, wasn't I?

Melania — You were great.

Donald — That's so relaxing when you say that. When you tell me things like that... I sleep better.

Melania — I've noticed.

Donald — Do you realize the political implications of that statement?

Melania — What do you mean?

Donald — Better sleep, better judgment... you may just keep me from starting a war... simply because of your loving me with all your sweetness...

She rests her head on his shoulder.

Donald — So, don't you ever think that you lack political clout...
you do, sweetie pie... oh, you do so much.
Melania — Dee...
Donald — Yes...?
Melania — Do think about what I said... please.
Donald — I will... I promise.
Melania — Just one term... and let's go back home.

2/24/17 — Trump tweets—FAKE NEWS media knowingly doesn't tell the truth. A great danger to our country. The failing @nytimes has become a joke. Likewise @CNN. Sad!

2/25 — Trump tweets—Maybe the millions of people who voted to MAKE AMERICA GREAT AGAIN should have their own rally. It would be the biggest of them all!

2/25 — He tweets—The media has not reported that the National Debt in my first month went down by $12 billion vs a $200 billion increase in Obama first mo.

2/25 — He tweets—Great optimism for future of U.S. business, AND JOBS, with DOW having an 11th straight record close. Big tax and regulation coming!

2/25 — He tweets—Congratulations to Thomas Perez, who has just been named Chairman of the DNC. I could not be happier for him, or for the Republican Party!

2/25 — He tweets—The race for DNC Chairman was, of course, totally "rigged." Bernie's guy, like Bernie himself, never had a chance. Clinton demanded Perez!

2/26 — He tweets—Russia talk is FAKE NEWS put out by the Dems, and played up by the media, in order to mask the big election defeat and the illegal leaks!

5

They're both sitting at the table in the bedroom. Donald is looking off, sometimes glancing at the ceiling, sometimes nodding to himself. Melania is reading the newspaper. A bottle of fine apple cider and two half filled glasses stand in the center of the table.

Donald — I have an idea.
Melania — What?
Donald — I've decided to get myself a woman doctor.

Amused, she puts the paper down.

Melania — Why?
Donald — I read somewhere that it's better for my health.
Melania — How come?
Donald — Because women are better communicators.

She smiles.

Donald — So... I'll have to let my old doc go. You think he'll mind?
Melania — Of course he will.
Donald — We'll stay friends, of course... bring him down to Mar-a-Lago now and then, all expenses paid. But I need to be pragmatic. A woman doctor will not only be better for my health but also for my image. 'First Woman to be The Personal Doctor of a Sitting President', how does that sound?
Melania — Impressive.
Donald — Another first for the Donald. When a woman academic writes a history of feminism, I'll have my name in there. I can see the headlines, 'President Trump Breaks with Tradition and Opens Up Opportunities for Women'. Something like that.
Melania — That's the beauty of being in office, isn't it, gives you all the options.

Donald — And that's just the beginning.

Melania — What else?

Donald — I'm going to promote more women to the rank of general.

Melania — Your ratings will improve. For sure. Just don't try to grope them.

Donald — Melania!

Melania — I've forgiven you enough, Dee. But I won't keep doing it.

Donald — Thank you. Like I told you, that chapter in my life is closed. You have nothing to worry about.

Melania — Hope so.

Donald — I wonder, though, whether a woman general has ever been groped?

Melania — Stop!

Donald — While in uniform...

Melania — Stop!!

Donald — It was just a thought.

Melania — I will not hear about it again. I'm warning you.

Donald — I got it. I'm not promoting them for the ratings, although that would be a bonus. I'm doing it for the principle.

Melania — I hope so.

Donald — They might bring a softer touch to the war business.

Melania — Women can be just as tough as men, if they have to.

Donald — Hmm. You're happy with your doctor?

Melania — She's great. I'm keeping her.

Donald — Glad to hear it. I couldn't stand you having a man doctor.

Melania — Why?

Donald — That's just me. Another man touching you? Nope, no siree.

Melania — Silly. You know I adore you.

Donald — It's the principle of it. (he looks at her) You're not worried about a woman doctor touching me?

Melania — Not really.

Donald — I'm offended.

Melania — Okay, I am. Just a little. What age should she be?

Donald — Have not thought about that.

Melania — I prefer that she be very seasoned.

Donald — Of course.

Melania — Much older than you.

Donald — No doubt.

Melania — Not sexy.

Donald — All business.

Melania — Exactly.

Clasping his hands, smiling, he stretches his arms up in the air.

Donald — I love it in here.

Melania — It's very nice. What do you like the most about being in the White House?

Donald — That the whole world is watching me. Every day, every minute. Like being on Reality TV. Hmm. Which makes me wonder...

Melania — What?

Donald — I just got another idea.

Melania — Let's hear it.

Donald — What if I delivered a summary of world events every week, live on TV?

Melania — In place of your Saturday weekly address?

Donald — That, and to replace the press briefings, which are a nuisance. I'm talking an hour-long program.

Melania — An hour may be too long. You might trip over yourself. Your grasp of policy details is not your strength.

Donald — It's getting better. We'd call it...'The Oval Office, brought to you by Colgate and Winchell's'. Another first for a sitting president. And I would just tell it like it is, the way only Donald can. People wouldn't have to bother reading the newspapers. No more fake news. And when Shinzo was in town, or Vlady, or Angie, or Theresa, or Xi, why I'd have them on the show, too. And the American people would get to know them. And the world would be a better, happier place. And you can be the producer and have a part in it. For instance, during a break, you could take a few minutes to familiarize ordinary people with the White House. Show them the kitchen, the dining room, how to prepare a recipe you might come up with, or you might interview the servants so they can tell their stories. We can get a dog, also. Just not a Portuguese Water dog. And maybe you can have a segment in the show where you play with it. Go, Hussein, go! Fetch the stick, boy!

Melania — Hussein?

Donald — Obama's middle name.

Melania — That's not funny.

Donald — My, my, we can't joke in private? Lighten up, okay?

Melania — I'm sorry.

Donald — (reaching over, taking her hand and kissing it) Forgiven.

Melania — Thank you.

Donald — See, dear, I understand media. And that's no idle claim, either. I spent a lot less than Hillary and landed us here. And the more I get to know Washington, the more I'll learn about how to get the right message out. It may be early, but I'm forecasting that I will win the next term.

She is silent.

Donald — And maybe even a third one... if I can change the rules.

Melania — You can't.

Donald — That's what they said about my chances of winning.

Melania — You can't change that rule.

Donald — Imagine that. Me in my 80s, being President of the United States of America. That would be another first right there, no one's been President while in their 80s. And the Trump brand flying higher than ever, higher than Apple, higher than Google. My hotels filled with people.

Melania — The world your stage.

Donald — It's addicting... this being in the spotlight.

Melania — You've always loved the spotlight, ever since I met you.

Donald — What attracted you to me? I'd just like to hear it again.

Melania — Your energy. Your lust for power.

Donald — Thank you.

They look at each other smilingly.

Donald — I love you so much. Sometimes I get mad and I say things that don't make sense, but then I recover. And I do because underneath it all, I'm happy. And I'm happy because of you.

She blows him a kiss.

Donald — You know, there's something else I've already done for this nation but I've yet to get credit for.
Melania — What's that?
Donald — I have made the Office of the Presidency accessible to all Americans.
Melania — How so?
Donald — They see me and they realize they're a little like me. Flawed. Imperfect. And that motivates them. They see me, and don't think I'm better than them—richer yes, but not better—so they believe they can do it, too. I inspire them.
Melania — They can have a beer with you...
Donald — Look how I've got everybody talking politics, everybody energized and giving an opinion. They won't come out and say it, but deep down they're grateful I've mobilized their emotions. Deep down they're grateful I have stirred life in them.
Melania — The Trump magic?
Donald — There you go. And that anger the democrats have for me...
Melania — It runs deep...
Donald — ...it comes from not wanting to come to terms with the truth.
Melania — What truth?
Donald — That I am a man of the people. They claimed to be for the people and here I come, a republican, and a filthy rich one, too, and I steal that claim from them in broad daylight. Just snatch it away.
Melania — I'm sure someone is writing the script of your rise to power... as we speak.
Donald — I had not thought about that. Thank you, Melania. That would be a kick in the pants, wouldn't it? Would you like to produce?
Melania — No.

Donald — You can always change your mind. But back to those hopeless democrats. The anger that is consuming them is pure self hatred. Because they didn't recognize—from the very beginning—that I was *the* man of the people. And I may have been ornery, crude on occasion, vicious, impulsive, thoughtless, even gropey...

Melania — Stop it!

Donald — Sorry. A clown now and then, sure—not that I take offense—but I was never mightier than thou. And I always made them laugh and when you do that you're a man of the people. (he smiles) I brought humor to the campaign.

Melania — That you did.

Donald — And I've brought humor to the Office of President.

She says nothing as she fills the glasses with cider.

Melania — (raising her glass) To humor.

Donald — Cheers!

Now he offers a toast,

Donald — To the Trump magic... to the Trump spell... to three terms in office... to breaking the rules!

They both drink. He stares at her.

Donald — How come you didn't say cheers?

Melania — Your polls are down.

Donald — Those are the same pollsters who had Hillary winning by a wide margin.

He gets up and strides over to the window.

Donald — What people have trouble realizing is that I will do or say anything to stay on top. And what does it take to pull that off?

Melania — A terrific actor.

Donald — Beautiful. And sooner or later everybody will love me, even Hollywood, although they won't be honest about it. But I don't exactly care for that crowd so it's their loss. They won't be coming to Mar-a-Lago to play golf with me, or the White House, that's for sure. But it does bug me that I don't get credit for my power to entertain. Because I can do that. I can make people laugh.

Melania — To be able to laugh at yourself, that's even better.

He turns to look at her.

Donald — You don't think I can laugh at myself?

Melania — No. You're too sensitive to criticism.

Donald — (nods, pensively) I have to work on that.

He returns to the table and sits.

Melania — I've been meaning to ask you...

Donald — Anything sweetheart, anything.

Melania — You know what I'd really like?

Donald — Just say it.

Melania — My security detail...

Donald — Your presidential escort, you mean?

Melania — I like the sound of it.

Donald — What about it... you're not pleased?

Melania — Oh, I am... it's just that... I was wondering... I'd like for it to be all women.

Donald — What?

Melania — I'd like that.

Donald — No. And that's N—O. It wouldn't be safe.

Melania — I'm sure there are enough strong women out there to keep me safe wherever I go.

Donald — You're asking too much.

Melania — Think of it. Every time I'd go out I would be making a statement for women... and for your presidency.

Donald — Where did this come from?

Melania — It just occurred to me the other day.

Donald — Who were you talking to?

Melania — I have ideas, too.

Donald — Of course. (reluctantly) I can't promise anything but I'll consider it.

Melania — And there's something else...

Donald — We need to go easy with the changes.

Melania — I'd like to have another child.

Donald — (baffled) You're not serious?

Melania — I am.

Donald — But... *can* you?

Melania — I beg your pardon... can *you*?

Donald — Of course I can.

Melania — Wouldn't that be wonderful? A baby born in the White House. I'm thrilled with the possibility. And I'd like for the baby to be a girl.

Donald — (chuckling) You're not thinking of running for office, too?

Melania — I can't run for president, of course...

Donald — True.

Melania — ... but I wouldn't mind starting a political party.

Donald — (incredulous) What?

Melania — To enliven the debate.

He laughs.

Donald — (with an air of condescension) You do have a sense of humor. And what party would that be, dear?

Melania — The WP.

Donald — Ha! The Workers' Party.

Melania — No, the Women's Party.

Donald — (frowning) Too polarizing. I never thought of you having political ambitions.

Melania — That's the thing about being close to power... it gives you ideas. That's why it was important for women to vote for Hillary.

Donald — Let's not go back to that. Did you vote for her?

Melania smiles slyly.

Donald — We'll never know, will we?

Most of the world's nations have never had a female leader—Pew Research Center.

2/27/17 — Trump tweets—Great meeting with CEOs of leading U.S. health insurance companies who provide great healthcare to the American people.

3/2 — Trump tweets—Since November 8th, Election Day, the Stock Market has posted $3.2 trillion in GAINS and consumer confidence is at a 15 year high. Jobs!

The unemployment rate now is less than 5%, down from 10% in 2009.
(Didn't happen overnight)

3/2 — He tweets—Jeff Sessions is an honest man. He did not say anything wrong. He could have stated his response more accurately. But it was clearly not…

cont — … intentional. This whole narrative is a way of saving face for Democrats losing an election that everyone thought they were supposed…

cont — … to win. The Democrats are overplaying their hand. They lost the election, and now they have lost their grip on reality. The real story…

cont- … is all of the illegal leaks of classified and other information. It is a total "witch hunt!"

Gallup Daily: Trump Job Approval—51% disapprove, while 43% approve.

6

They're sitting at the table in their bedroom. Melania is in her night gown, browsing a magazine. His phone is on the table.

Melania — We should clear the air.
Donald — About what?
Melania — It was hard for me, during the campaign, to hear all those things you said about women.
Donald — I'm sorry.
Melania — But I understood.
Donald — I'm glad.
Melania — That sometimes you're a jerk.

He glances at her, then nods.

Donald — (a tad remorseful) That's true.
Melania — And I understood, because you do not mistreat me... and if you ever do I will put you in your place. So I understood.
Donald — Thank you, baby.
Melania — I understood the difference between your public persona and the private one. And that you lack a certain polish...
Donald — Now hold on....
Melania — Don't interrupt me.
Donald — I'm sorry.
Melania — You lack a certain finesse... but I have seen you be a good father to Ivanka and to our son and that says a lot to me.
Donald — I knew you'd understand.
Melania — And I'd rather know the truth about you than you be a hypocrite.
Donald — You're the best, sweetie pie.
Melania — Sometimes you behave like a caveman and you think it's funny... but it's not. And I'm glad I'm bringing this up because, after you said those things, you did not apologize to me.

Donald — (protesting) I didn't say them to you…
Melania — You said them to women, and because I am a woman and your wife, and the mother of your son, you need to come home and apologize to me.
Donald — Okay, I see your point.

She sits back and folds her arms. He looks at her, a bit puzzled. After a moment of silence, he begins again.

Donald — I'm glad you got that off your chest. It certainly was a busy week, don't you think? Did you enjoy reading to the children?

She says nothing.

Donald — Baby…everything okay?
Melania — I'm waiting…
Donald — Oh… of course… I apologize.

She remains in her same posture.

Donald — (sighing, crossing his arms over his head) Look, I'm not good at guessing… just tell me what I have to do.
Melania — Do a formal apology.
Donald — Why formal?
Melania — Because it's a serious issue.
Donald — Do I have to get on my knees?
Melania — I'm not telling you what to do, you're a grown man.

Reluctantly, he gets up and standing before her, eases himself down to his knees. He has to lean on the edge of the table to assist himself—but he does it.

Donald — (a bit miffed) Do not let this get out, you hear me? If you write a memoir do not put this in, okay?

She looks at him but says nothing.

Donald — I apologize...

Melania — Formally...

Donald — I formally apologize... (he hesitates) for all the nasty things I've said about women... and the things I might say about women...

Melania — No. That won't work. You can't apologize in advance.

He begins to get up but she stops him.

Melania — Stay!

Donald — Please! My knees are killing me!

Melania — You have to lose weight. Start again.

Donald — (speaking rapidly) I formally apologize for all the nasty things I've said about women. Now...

She stares down at him.

Donald — That good enough for you?

Melania — No. You rushed the lines... there was no meaning behind them.

Donald — (pleading) Melania, baby, I am serious, my knees are going... they'll have to push me around in a wheelchair... it won't be good for the country... I will not project an image of strength... I'll be cranky and might make a mistake and start a war.

Melania — (not persuaded) Start all over.

Donald — Please, honey... I beg you... (now clearly upset) this is the President of the United States begging you!

Melania — (unimpressed) Start all over.

Donald — (reluctantly taking a moment to compose himself, head bowed) I formally apologize to you, Melania Knauss Trump, a strong woman, an immigrant from Slovenia, but a naturalized citizen of the United States, who speaks five languages...

Melania — You don't have to go into all that...

Donald — Okay...for all the crude things I said about women... during the campaign... and before the campaign... and I vow... (he halts for a moment)

Melania — Go on...

Donald — ... to make my very best effort to be kind and thoughtful... even if I don't agree with what women—democrats mainly—may say and think about me...

Melania — Please include all women.

Donald — ...even if I don't agree with what women—democrats or republican—may say about me.

Melania — You left out independents, but good. This time I believed you.

He remains kneeling, head bowed. She takes his phone from the table and puts it in her pocket.

Melania — You can get up now

Donald — I can't.

Melania — What's wrong?

Donald — My knees won't let me. Call the National Security Advisor.

She gets up from her chair, stands up behind him and placing her arms under his armpits...

Melania — One, two... three!

Donald — (she gives him a good heave and with his holding on to the table, he pushes himself up) Owwww!!!

Melania — Don't be so dramatic.

She leads him to his chair where he plops down. Now she kneels next to him and starts to gently massage his knees.

Melania — There... you'll feel better in a minute.

Donald — Thank you.

He caresses her head.

Donald — Actually... I feel cleansed...

Melania — I knew it would be good for you... I know you can change.

Donald — I'm glad you have the confidence. But just so you know… now and then… in the fury of the moment… I may say some things…

Melania — Then you'll have to apologize all over again, won't you?

Donald — I'll try.

Melania — Until you get it right. (brief pause) I am the first lady. I take my official duties very seriously.

Donald — Listen to me, I'm serious, too. If I have to keep doing this you'll make me have a knee replacement… I'll have to be under anesthesia… which means I'll have to temporarily cede power…

Melania — Mike will take over.

Donald — Mike…?

Melania — Mike Pence.

Donald — Absolutely not. I'll ask them to give me a spinal instead.

Melania — Don't worry, you won't need a knee replacement.

Donald — Help me lose the weight, sweetheart… please.

Melania — You never put it that way.

Donald — I'm asking you, seriously.

She gets up and returns to her seat.

Melania — We can start walking together tomorrow morning.

Donald — Where?

Melania — Down in the gym.

Donald — Haven't been down there yet.

Melania — And there's a very cool exercise bike, too. We'll go step by step. Eventually, you'll get to do chin-ups. Like Obama.

Donald — You're putting too much pressure on me.

Melania — Okay, we'll stick to the walking.

Donald — Good. (pausing) Hmm… I just had another idea… imagine me losing the weight and boosting the dialogue about obesity in America. Imagine what that will do for my ratings?

Melania — That would be an incentive.

Donald — It just occurred to me. That's how I get all my ideas, you know, in the spur of the moment.

Melania — You need to think more long term.

Donald — I'm an impulse kind of guy. It's a different kind of thinking. Call it visceral—thinking with the gut—and you don't have to do too much worrying, either, until after the fact. It's thinking in the open, publicly, not afraid to show your flaws. People react and you counter react and so on. Hmmm. I should write a book about that. But really, me losing weight on prime time, isn't it brilliant? I would be setting an example and saving the lives of millions and millions of people. Imagine all those folks who are on their way to becoming diabetic, and how dieting with me would turn their lives around… and they would be able to say that I helped save their lives… and they would be voting again when I run for re-election.

Melania — But what if you can't do it?

Donald — What kind of talk is that? Of course I can do it.

Melania –You'll have to eat less meat. And what are the cattle ranchers to say about that?

Donald — It might have an impact on the commodities market… is that what you're saying?

Melania — Yes. You'd be getting a lot of calls…

Donald — From people who like me nice and fat…

She gives him a slow nod.

Melania — When you're in the spotlight… there are pluses and minuses.

Donald — But I need to lose weight.

Melania — I agree. So you have to make a choice.

Donald — Didn't Bush the Elder get a lot of flak for saying he didn't like broccoli?

Melania — I remember that.

Donald — You know… let them deal with it… I can't be worrying about everybody. However… I'm starting to see some commercial possibilities here. What if we began by designing the kinds of meals I should be eating… the calories per day… giving ourselves a time limit… say 60 days… 'The Trump 60 day Diet'. We could market that.

Melania — 100 days might be better.

Donald — You don't trust me, do you?

Melania — Better give ourselves some room.

Donald — Okay, and we'll write the book together. 'The Trump 100 day Power Diet'. I'm already seeing publishers falling over each other to give us an advance. And we'll serve the menus in the hotels, worldwide. 'President Trump's Diet'. Don't you love it already?

Melania — It could also be the 'Donald and Melania Diet'.

Donald — Of course, but I think my idea has more oomph. But we can leave that for later. The point is, here's another example of the fact that a man can make a lot of money and still do good. Like I have with my brand.

Melania — Are you serious about the weight loss?

Donald — I am.

Melania — I like it also because it might help us have the baby.

Donald — Hmm. It would help the ratings...

Melania — True... in which case... we could try for two...

Donald — Two instead of one?

Melania — Exactly.

They look at each other for a moment. She winks at him. He winks back.

Donald — I wonder where I put my phone...

Melania — I have it.

Donald — Hand it over.

Melania — No.

Donald — Honey, don't do this to me... you know you're interfering with matters of state, don't you?

Melania — Am I?

She rises and then slowly starts to sashay her way to the bed while letting her gown slide, seductively, off her shoulders.

Melania — (smiling enticingly over her shoulder) Well, then, matters of state will have to wait, won't they, big boy?

Donald — (his eyes wide, his lust piqued) Yes... Yes!

News — FBI director James Comey testified to
Congress in 2014, that "violent extremists do
not share a typical profile: their experiences and
motives are often distinct."

"There have been no fatalities in the United States
caused by extremists with family backgrounds in
Iraq, Iran, Libya, Somalia, Sudan, Syria, Yemen
(the countries affected by the travel suspension). —
Charles Klurzman, Dept of Sociology, University of
North Carolina, Chapel Hill. 1/26/2017 -

3/4/17 — Trump tweets—Terrible! Just found out
that Obama had my "wires tapped" in Trump Tower
just before the victory. Nothing found. This is
McCarthyism!

3/4 — He tweets—How low has President Obama gone
to tap my phones during the very sacred election
process. This is Nixon/Watergate. Bad (or sick) guy!

3/4 — He tweets—Arnold Schwarzenegger isn't volun-
tarily leaving the Apprentice, he was fired by his
bad (pathetic) ratings, not by me. Sad end to a
great show

1/29/17 — Shooting at a mosque in Quebec City,
Canada, leaves 6 dead and 8 wounded. The shooter,
a university student, was described as having far
right views. The victims were praying when struck
by the bullets.

2/3/17 — The Museum of Modern Art presents an
exhibit of works by artists from the majority
Muslim countries affected by Trump's travel suspension, "to affirm the ideals of welcome and freedom

as vital to this Museum as they are to the United
States."

3/4/17 — Gallup Daily: Trump Job Approval - 53%
disapprove while 42% approve.

7

Sitting at the table in their bedroom. Evening.

Melania — I don't understand.

Donald — It's a promise I made and I have to keep. That simple.

Melania — Did you ever have a problem with a Muslim person?

Donald — Not at all.

Melania — Because a few people have been violent you blame an entire faith.

Donald — It could happen any moment and then... what am I going to say?

Melania — You can't control everything. Any moment we could have a zealot or demented person throw a bomb into our garden.

Donald — Hope not.

Melania — But we would have to look at the person to find out what happened to him, or her, that they gave up on the chance of living a life. I am sure that person was not born to be a bomb thrower.

Donald — They train them from when they're toddlers.

Melania — You don't know that.

Donald — I'm convinced that's what they do.

Melania — It's only the extremists and they're a very small minority.

Donald — Whatever. I will not let them through.

Melania — It's overkill. You're doing what Bush did when he ordered the invasion of Iraq.

Donald — How so?

Melania — All along we had the technology to contain Saddam... but we didn't check and recheck the CIA's claim that he had weapons of mass destruction... so we rushed in and it was overkill. Look at the suffering...

Donald — That was 2003, Melania. And, by the way, Hillary voted in favor.

Melania — Not one of her best moments.

Donald — People have become more radicalized...

Melania — Which is why we need leadership, people who think.

Donald — ... Look what happened in Boston, in San Bernardino, in Orlando?

Melania — Would that have happened if we hadn't invaded Iraq?

Donald — I don't know. All I know is I have to deal with the world as it is now. And we need to cast a wide net, wide enough to catch those devils.

Melania — Devils?

Donald — Who else would try to hurt innocent Americans?

Melania — Who would want to hurt anyone? You don't have to be a devil, you have to be sick! Sick in the head! Sick in the heart! Why frame the argument in religious terms?

Donald — It's easier.

Melania — Really?

He stops, gets up, paces the room for a moment, then returns to face her at the table.

Donald — Look, political expedience is a fact of life. You think I'm being rash? I have a precedent.

Melania — Who?

Donald — One of our own, one of our best.

Melania — Who?

Donald — Franklin Delano Roosevelt. Japan attacked us... then all Japanese in the West Coast went straight to special camps. He did what he had to do and worried about the flak later.

Melania — Isn't it our task to learn from our mistakes? Surely there were other ways to address our security concerns.

Donald — Political expedience will never go out of style. You don't seem to grasp the concept.

Melania — Oh, I grasp it all right, I just think it's immoral.

Donald — Ha! Let me spell it out for you. Yes, I said some outlandish things during the campaign. But those outlandish things fired up a whole lot of people who were feeling they'd been left behind. I'm talking about red blooded Americans who

had been getting the shaft, people who were depressed and
in a stupor and banging their heads against a brick wall, and I
came along and got their attention and they started listening.
I raised hell and people woke up and you and I are having this
conversation in this beautiful room. How 'bout that?

Melania — Yes, the poor in your base were getting the shaft, but
wasn't it other Americans, just as white as they are, and rich like
you—and who were piling up the profits from globalization—who
didn't bother to check in with their brothers and sisters, see how
their communities were being affected? And I don't recall you
starting up an effort to address their concerns when the damage
was being done. No. Their plight—the plight of the poor in your
base—became your concern only when you needed a platform to
run for office, not before.

Donald — (calmly) If you're calling me a one percenter you need
to look at yourself, because you're a one percenter, also, so don't
be a hypocrite.

Melania — I'm trying to think, Dee, think out loud, isn't that what
you do?

He walks over to the window and gazes out.

Melania — (gently) You don't have to invent demons... be they
Muslims, Mexicans or whatever. The greater harm done to
poorer Americans, no matter what their color, and that includes
your base, comes from being neglected by the better off, who
don't think their brothers and sisters are capable of improving
themselves. And you're not addressing that.

Donald — Yes, I am.

They are quiet for a moment.

Melania — Not that your base doesn't bear its share of
responsibility. They lacked initiative, didn't organize, didn't
complain loud enough or long enough... and missed the warning
that they had to learn new skills to stay competitive.

He returns to the table and sits.

Donald — I'm not insensitive… or I am sometimes… but it's not like I don't see the big picture. And I grant… right now… some people will get hurt… but I will make adjustments.

Melania — For the sake of our security, the measures Obama had put in place are working…

Donald — Believe what you wish but I do not, let me be very clear—do not—want to be woken up to be told that some Muslim detonated a bomb in Times Square. So if some people will get hurt with the ban, so be it. The ban goes. It's been blocked twice but eventually I'll get it passed. I'll take it right up to the Supreme Court. And what's more, I'm thinking of getting it to be even more stringent. Did you see my budget proposals?

Melania—I did.

Donald — Up on defense, up on homeland security, up on veterans' affairs. Putting my money where my mouth is.

Melania — Those lives you're affecting are just as important as American lives.

Donald — They are not. Obama thinks they are, but what's his middle name? And where was he born?

Melania — That's nonsense and you know it.

Donald — He didn't put red blooded American lives first. He should've put in drastic measures after the bombings…

Melania — Like a Muslim ban? Built a wall?

Donald — … And he didn't because he's thinking global…thinking that a human from a Muslim country is the same as a human from America. He's not.

Melania — You don't really believe that, do you?

Donald — Honey, what got me to this office was the belief that we're special, plain and simple.

Melania — Dee… the *we* you're talking about is a mixture of the whole world. And so are the mothers of your children. Ivanka's mother is Czech born, I'm from Slovenia…

Donald — I'm not denying that we're a melting pot… what I'm affirming is that, in this moment in history, whoever got melted has melted enough, and that until there's peace in the world we're going to set limits. When will that happen is anybody's guess. But for now, we're having to retrench because it will be good for us. It will be good for us so we can clean up our house and reassert ourselves as the greatest. And so, for the time being, I'm pausing on the global thinking.

Melania — That's not the path for exceptional people.

Donald — We'll see about that.

Melania — Our riches have come from vigorous interaction with all nations, from being in everybody's business, sometimes for good and sometimes for ill, but we've been in the mix, not afraid of getting burnt and learning from it.

Donald — It's America First from now on. Heck of a slogan, too.

Melania — We've made mistakes. I read that, to help Colombia's economy and deter the cultivation of coca, we made it easier for flower growers to export and sell here in the U.S. But we hurt our own flower growers.

Donald — That's what I'm talking about.

Melania — But we don't have to shut down our nation's openness to the rest of the world to help the base. They need to be included in the process of transformation... not sheltered from it. They need to learn to dance to a different tune, to learn new steps because what we have now is a whole different gig.

Donald — I'm willing to learn, but for now...

Melania — Dee, you're shirking from complexity and appealing to emotion to go backwards... you're being atavistic and totemic.

Donald — Ha! Atavistic and totemic... I've been called some things but not that.

Melania — America has never been greater that it is now. And that's because we're being inclusive and diverse. All your talk about being great again is simply you selling snake oil.

Donald — We'll see.

Melania — And to make matters worse, you're being very smug about it.

Donald — A President is entitled to his moments.

Melania — Not if I have something to say about it.

Donald — Since when...

He pauses briefly.

Melania — You're being bull headed and dead wrong about insisting on the ban and I will not go along with you and will take my stand against it.
Donald — (mockingly) Knock yourself out.
Melania — You think I'm joking?
Donald — What're you going to do, write an op-ed article for that fake news rag in New York?
Melania — No. Better than that. I am going to convert to Islam.
Donald — (nearly falling out of his chair, with great alarm) What?
Melania — That's right. That way you will experience it firsthand.
Donald — Oh my God.

She's looking directly at him, unflinching.

Donald — Now come on, honey, let's not make a scene. You can't be serious?
Melania — Oh but I am. I will do that and start learning Spanish also. I've always wanted to learn an extra language, anyway. That will be my sixth.
Donald — Sweetheart... think... use your head for a moment... what will the whole world say... they'll think I'm weak... that I can't govern my own wife...
Melania — What? You think that a wife is to be governed?
Donald — Now, don't get all flustered, I didn't mean it that way.
Melania — How did you mean it?
Donald — It will give the wrong impression...
Melania — So be it. Let the world know that a wife is entitled to her own opinions, and that marriage is a partnership of equals. That my work at home as a mother is as valuable as yours, for I am helping shape a life...
Donald — Melania, stop!
Melania — If the spouses in your base would've believed in that, they would not have voted to please their husbands.

They stop and stare at each other.

Donald — (sounding hurt) You wanted Hillary to win, didn't you?
Melania — I believe in you, Dee... I want you to succeed... and I will battle at your side till the end. I just do not agree with your invoking political expedience to run over people, and so I must voice my opinion. I will not concede on that.
Donald — Melania, I've told you... these are temporary measures... just to please the base... I'll change things later.
Melania — You just don't get it. (she drops her face in her hands for a moment, then, looking at him again, speaking calmly and with determination) I'll ask Ivanka to design some robes for me. I can only imagine the impact that will have... worldwide... Ivanka being Jewish and me Muslim, and us getting along perfectly well. How it will affect the peace process in the Middle East.
Donald — My God, you've gone berserk! No, it won't. People will think it's a stunt, that we're mocking them. Putin will have a stroke, and Netanyahu will have a heart attack... or vice versa, and I won't have a chance in hell to get re-elected.
(he stops)
Wait, scratch that. I won this election on my own.
Melania — We'll have to wait and see, won't we?
Donald — I beg of you... please reconsider.
Melania — Just doing my wifely duties, no more, no less. Fulfilling my role as first lady of this nation.

She gets up and goes to the window.

Melania — It's a whole new world out there and I'm not going to retreat from it.
Donald — Look, just because you're my wife I don't have to take your advice.
Melania — You're free to take it or not. And I'm free to give it.
Donald — I do not understand what's got into you? You used to be so agreeable....
Melania — Agreeable, hunh?
Donald — I mean, without these political affectations... who have you been talking to?

Melania — Affectations you call them... fancy word. No, Dee... I'm being vocal, that's all. No more me just thinking and keeping it to myself. No more Melania being the wallpaper in the room. I will have an opinion and I will express it.

Donald — Excuse me but, were you elected?

Melania — No. I was not. But I'm going to have my opinions anyway. Someone has to burst your bubble. And I don't tweet.

Donald — You're behaving like a child, not like a true first lady.

Melania — Well, the concept is evolving and you'll just have to learn to adapt.

He gets up and goes to join her by the window.

Donald — Melania...I have a show to run...

Melania — Not a show Dee... you have a nation to lead.

Donald — Will you please let me finish?

They are quiet for a moment.

Donald — I need peace and quiet at home... it is very simple... a massage after work... my toe nails clipped now and then...

Melania — You're missing the point. This is a very special moment in history and I'm not going to spend it as an ornament in the White House. And I can still get you your slippers. And clip your toenails.

Donald — (furious) I'll get my own damned slippers!

Melania — Good.

Donald — (controlling himself) Melania... just because you're sharing my bed... I am not obligated to listen to your half baked political opinions.

She steps forward and throws wide open the drapes on the window.

Donald — Why did you do that?

Melania — Because we need more light in this room... light and air so you can clear the cobwebs in your mind.

Donald — (deeply annoyed, gesturing with his arms) If I had known you would be acting this way, I would've left you in New York!

Melania — (opening the leaves of the tall windows) I need to breathe...

Donald — It's Michelle, isn't it?

Melania — Michelle?

Donald — Your new role model?

Melania — (calmly) I suppose we all need role models... but it's not Michelle... smart as she is.

Donald — Who is it, then?

Melania — You really want to know?

Donald — Yes!

Melania — Angela Merkel.

He raises his hands in exasperation.

Melania — You know why?

Donald — I don't care!

Melania — Because she had the guts to accept all those Syrian refugees. Even if it may cost her her job.

Donald — You've become a lunatic. I don't recognize you anymore. Who are you?

Melania — I am a thinking woman and proud of it.

Donald — Look, this has got to stop!

Melania — Why do you think this country has not elected an unmarried man to be President in well over a century?

Donald — Why Melania?

Melania — Because they understand the balance that a woman brings to a President.

Donald — That is pure speculation on your part, just plain hogwash.

Melania — The nation understands that, in his private moments, a President needs the tonic a good wife will bring.

Donald — Okay, then, where's the tonic? I don't see it! If you have it, let me get drunk with it. But, as of right now, all I'm getting from you is grief! Where the hell is the tonic!?

Melania — (turning to face him squarely) I am giving it to you but you're not getting it. Instead you're carrying on as if you were running the hotel business. And I am here to act as your reality check. You are now the 45th President of the United States, so start acting like it!

Donald — I have a mandate to make us great again.

Melania — No, you don't. You lost the popular vote by nearly three million votes...

Donald — Those votes were fraudulent.

Melania — ... And if American women had not been in the habit of deferring to their spouses, you would not have been elected. And women have been in that habit of deferring because it has been beat into them.

Donald — So you did vote for Hillary, didn't you?

Melania — (grabbing him by the shirt, angrily) I cannot believe that you do not know in your bones who I voted for.

Donald — Why can't you just tell me?

Melania — Because I shouldn't have to.

Donald — I know you voted for her.

She turns away from him and returns to gazing out the window.

Donald — This betrayal of yours, I can't believe it.

Melania — Betrayal you say? You know what really would be betrayal? For me to just go along with you. *That* would be betrayal.

Brief pause.

Melania — Something new and beautiful started to happen in our country with the election of Barack... and neither you nor your base can see it. He was not perfect, he made his mistakes... Syria, North Korea... maybe even the handling of Russia's hacking our emails... but his election and presidency marked a new beginning. White America played the decisive role in winning World War II and ushered in a new world order, and we will always be indebted to them because with their sacrifice they gave us liberty, but the

world goes on and we have a new dynamic. But you... you want the country to go back to that time. Well, it can't be done.
Donald — We'll see about that. It is me proposing the budget increases for defense, homeland and veterans' affairs, not you, dear.
Melania — You can't just militarize the work force. We're about much more than that. I thought about what you said the other day... how you had energized the nation... but you're wrong. The nation is energized not because you enlightened it, it is up in arms for not having taken seriously the importance of their vote... their civic duty... and not seizing the moment to elect a woman.
Donald — You voted for her, didn't you? I knew it!
Melania — The nation is up in arms for not recognizing that you were atavistic and totemic...
Donald — Stop saying that, I hate it!
Melania — ... And realizing they now have to deal with the consequences of their mistake.
Donald — My base was ignored by Obama...
Melania — Yes it was. And by all the republican and democratic administrations that came before.
Donald — ... And I alone, Donald J Trump, was the one to seize the moment. I alone, carpe diem!

He moves forward to stand in the center of the window, ahead of Melania, and gaze out.

Melania — Yes. You alone stirred their rage... a rage filled with envy for those moving past in the struggle to improve themselves... a rage that you don't seem prepared to transform into a positive force.
Donald — I don't have to listen to all of that.

She shakes her head slowly. A moment passes. Then she advances toward him and puts her hand on his shoulder.

Donald — (calmly) You've said a lot of hurtful things... maybe you're not through.

Melania — I am.

She rubs his back and leans her head on his shoulder.

Melania — I care about you, Dee... and I've said what I said because I think you can do better.

He continues to silently look out the window, at the city and the world beyond.

Donald — I'm doing the best I can... do you believe that...?
Melania — I do...
Donald — I don't want to fail in front of so many people... in front of the whole world...
Melania — I feel that, Dee... I really do.

He lowers his head.

Donald — Sometimes... in the Oval Office... I feel very alone. I do realize that I'm being rash with all these tough stances I'm taking. I know the world we live in is more complicated than that... it's just that... the transition has been rough... more so than I expected... and maybe I'm in over my head. And I'm still finding the few men... and women... I can really trust... who want me to succeed... and are not just in it for themselves.
Melania — (putting her arm around him as both look front) You're smart, Dee... but you have to be more thoughtful... more of a gradualist... the base will stick with you if you explain that we have to move forward... that we have to embrace a brave new world... and we all need a dialogue that engages us... so we can better face the complexities that lie ahead.
Donald — I'm not sure I understand them myself.
Melania — It's a big job.

He puts his arm around her, holds her close to him for a moment.

Donald — Say, why don't you drop by the office sometime?

Melania — In the middle of the day?

Donald — Sure. (winks at her) I'll hang a Do Not Disturb sign on the door.

Melania — (smiling) I'll do that.

Donald — Looking forward to it.

Melania — But no cuchi cuchi.

Donald — Oh, c'mon.

Melania — Not in the Oval Office.

Donald — Not ever?

Melania — Okay, maybe late at night... when the world is at peace.

They kiss.

Donald — Maybe we can conceive a child there.

Melania — I don't know... I'll have to think about that.

Donald — Changing your mind already? You looked kind of cute with the big belly. And it might help the ratings.

She gives him a good, long squeeze.

Donald — You know what I just thought?

Melania — What?

Donald — Putting together a group of men and women, white, black, Hispanic, Asian... various ages... regular folks... from all over the nation... and have them come together to spend the day with me once a month... unless there's a crisis of course... so we can chat about the things that matter to them... just me and them... and they can tell me what they really think. You could come, too.

Melania — I like it. A different group every month?

Donald — Yeah. Twenty, thirty people. Picked through a national lottery. A dollar a ticket. Proceeds to pay for their expenses and the rest to go to charity. I just made that up, too.

Melania — I think it's brilliant. You just thought about it right now?

Donald — Yes. Right now, when you gave me that squeeze.

Melania — Wow. Squeeze, and out pops the idea. Just be sure they don't stay in your hotel.

Donald — A motel should do.

Melania — Save money.

Donald — We could call it the United America Lottery, the UAL.

Melania — UAL… hmm… (playfully) U Are Loco (you are mad).

Donald — Watch it, I know a little Spanish, too.

She squeezes him again.

Donald — Hey… and you know how Hillary had that Muslim woman who was a close aide?

Melania — Huma Abedin…

Donald — No, scratch that. That was not a good idea. Not everything that pops out of me is good.

Melania — True. But I could visit a mosque… it would send a message.

Donald — Skip the mosque for now.

Melania — It's a thought. I'll start by reading the Quran.

Donald — That's more like it. I've never read it.

They turn toward each other and kiss.

Donald — You think my getting elected was a fluke?

Melania — I do. But we'll make a go of it, won't we? And you'll make a good President. I'm committing to the one term.

Donald — One term, huh? I don't know about that.

Melania — One term, Dee… it's enough… and let's go back home and live our lives.

Donald — I'll think about it. (smiling) You in the mood…?

Melania — (cuddling up against him) I am.

3/7/17 — Trump tweets—Our wonderful new Healthcare
Bill is now out for review and negotiation.
ObamaCare is a complete and total disaster—is
imploding fast!

3/7 — He tweets—Don't worry, getting rid of state
lines, which will promote competition, will be in
phase 2 & 3 of healthcare rollout.

3/7 — He tweets—I am working on a new system where
there will be competition in the Drug industry.
Pricing for the American people will come way down!

3/7 — He tweets—Don't let FAKE NEWS tell you that
there is big infighting in the Trump Admin. We are
getting along great, and getting major things done!

3/7/17 — Trump tweets—For eight years Russia "ran
over" President Obama, got stronger and stronger,
picked off Crimea and added missiles. Weak!

3/8 — He tweets—I have tremendous respect for
women and the many roles they serve that are vital
to the fabric of our society and our economy.
(International Women's Day)

8

Donald is at the table, in his bathrobe, eyes on his phone. Melania is lying in bed, in her nightie, reading a book.

Melania — Why, Dee? There's no evidence that your phones were ever tapped.
Donald — Not so far, but it's coming.
Melania — Who put that bug in your head?
Donald — No one did. I just woke up one morning and there it was.
Melania — Was I here?
Donald — You were in New York.
Melania — And you took it and started tweeting on it.
Donald — Yep. I needed to get it off my chest.
Melania — It makes you look paranoid.
Donald — Maybe so.
Melania — The deep state?
Donald — Perhaps. You don't realize the extent to which I'm considered a threat to the status quo. I was elected to set another course for the nation. You need to understand that.
Melania — Another course, as in completely denying that climate change is an issue?
Donald — I have to see more evidence.
Melania — The entire world's scientific community, who has conducted extensive research and taken tons of measurements, doesn't know what they're talking about?
Donald — Need to help those boys in the coal mines. Focus on being great again.
Melania — Taking us out of the Paris accord on climate change?
Donald — Maybe.
Melania — But for sure there will be an increase in defense spending, more new weapons, right?
Donald — I keep my campaign promises.

Melania — And help the base dream of power.

Donald — Keeping them safe, Melania, keeping them safe. Don't be cynical.

Melania — It will do nothing to make them more competitive.

Donald — Give me some time on that. Meanwhile, building more weapons gives them something to be proud of.

Melania — You remind me of Kim Jong-un.

Donald — Do I?

Melania — Selling dreams of missiles for his personal aggrandizement and to distract the population from much needed reforms.

Donald — I'm going to send him an autographed copy of "The Art of The Deal." He might like it. We need to meet, we might just get along.

He starts a tweet. "Despite what you hear in the press, healthcare is coming along great. We are talking to many groups and it will end in a beautiful picture!"

Melania — Who are you tweeting?

Donald — The world. Now that I'm settling in, I'm having more fun being President. When I went to the Hill the other day, to put pressure on some folks to vote for the health care bill... and I told a few of them that they would lose their jobs if they didn't come on board... I felt that excitement again. The arm twisting, you know?

Melania — And you're doing it for your base?

Donald — Who else?

Melania — You think Kim Jong-un has a base?

Donald — Of course he does. He wouldn't be in power if he didn't. And he takes good care of it, too.

Melania — It takes a certain sleight of hand.

Donald — There you go. And that's where the Trump magic comes in.

Melania — I suppose I fell prey to it also.

Donald — No, sweetheart, you're special. I had to use my secret charms with you.

She laughs.

Melania — What about the people who now oppose you?
Donald — They'll come around.
Melania — More arm twisting?
Donald — They'll see the writing on the wall. I just have to concentrate on keeping my base happy and they'll do the work for me. And before you know it, everyone will be referring to me as Uncle Donald. As for the diehards, money in their pocket will turn them around. Notice how the markets keep moving up, not just here but globally?
Melania — I read that it takes about 8 years to recover completely from a financial crisis, and that's how long it's been since the subprime fiasco.
Donald — Melania, dear, please don't deny me that. Markets are going up because of me, because I've promised tax cuts and deregulation. I've inspired the movers and shakers of this nation, the elite, without which we would have nothing at all, the enterprising people, without which there would be no pie to slice.
Melania — And won't the deficit balloon out with the tax cuts?
Donald — (smiling broadly) I love debt. I adore it. If it weren't for debt, I wouldn't't've built my empire. Of course, now and then, you might have to file for bankruptcy.
Melania — I can only imagine the effect on the world markets... U.S.A. files for bankruptcy...

He laughs.

Donald — That will never happen.
Melania — Why not?
Donald — Because the world knows we're exceptional. The debt we'll go into, from the tax cuts, will finance the greatest growth the country has ever experienced... just like it has with my hotels... and the growth will be phenomenal... unheard of.
Melania — Just don't show the tax records.
Donald — Look, I've already talked to my accountant. I'll have a copy for you soon.

Melania — Thank you.

He puts the phone down.

Donald — Of course, if the economy starts tanking instead, for whatever reason, why there's always the option of starting a new war... somewhere. But that's standard.

Melania — We're kind of busy on that option, aren't we? Iraq... Afghanistan... supporting the freedom fighters in Syria...

Donald — I'm sure the extra spending will pull us up again.

Melania — Tax cuts and extra spending... knowledgeable people would say that's a recipe for disaster.

Donald — Melania, dear... I appreciate your enthusiasm but you're new to this.

Melania — You know what I've never heard you say... not even once...?

Donald — What's that?

Melania — That you want to invest in the people.

Donald — (a brief moment of reflection) Why, it's implicit. Of course I want to do that. That's what Trumpism is all about.

Melania — Is it? Okay, well, here's an idea for you.

Donald — Let's hear it.

Melania — Starting a department to promote better race relations.

Donald — We have enough bureaucracy already.

Melania — Listen to this. Years ago, I remember seeing a billboard that had two young children sitting side by side. They were maybe 5 or 6 years old and had their arms around each other as they faced front. One was white, the other black. The caption above read, 'prejudice is learned', or 'prejudice is taught'. I can't remember exactly. And it made quite an impression on me. Now, wouldn't that be investing in our nation, teaching, from pre- school and up, that we need to learn to accept and appreciate difference?

Donald — Parents would object.

Melania — But isn't that what good government is for— anticipating—spotting the obstacles ahead so we won't crash into them?

Donald — Very idealistic, but the party would be against it. We leave it up to the individual.
Melania — But if the individual isn't doing it, how do we move boldly into this century?
Donald — Even if I wanted to, I'd never get party support for it.
Melania — You could use your charm to sell it... use the bully pulpit...
Donald — It's not what my base is expecting from me.
Melania — But that's your job, to have vision... and then convince the people...
Donald — Melania... I'd have to be convinced myself... that's the problem.

She is quiet for a moment, the disappointment clear.

Melania — (more to herself) I'm so close to power and yet so far from it.
(then looking directly at him)
It brings back the idea of converting to Islam.

He looks down at the ground for a moment, then back at her.

Donald — It's not funny.
Melania — I'm not joking. We're living in challenging times, and you're not rising to the occasion. Our time needs a creative leader, one with the chutzpah to defy old beliefs and take us to new ground.
Donald — You're not going to pressure me into anything.
Melania — I don't want to pressure you, I want to jar you into finding your depth so you can lead.

He sighs, shakes his head disapprovingly.

Donald — You have really changed, haven't you?
Melania — (nodding softly) I have... and I'm glad.
Donald — You're not at all the same person you were when the campaign started.

Melania — No. But I love you just as much as I ever did... maybe even a little bit more... you know why?

Donald — Why?

Melania — Because you're flawed, just like me.

Donald — (rising from his seat) Goddammit! I want you to stop, right now!

He strides over to the window.

Donald — If it weren't because we're married, I would've fired you a long time ago.

Melania — One of the benefits of marriage.

Donald — It would be messy... and expensive... it's not like you're a tax deduction.

Melania — Thanks. But really, Dee, don't you appreciate my feedback?

Donald — Whatever it is, it's not feedback, it's something else... it's you trying to beat me up... punishing me for all those blunders I've made.

Melania — I'm sorry you see it that way.

He walks over to the closet and pulls out a coat.

Melania — Where are you going?

Donald — (as he puts on the coat) I'm not telling you. In fact, I may just stop talking to you for a while. Or move out to another room.

Melania — I could go into a silent mode... if you'd like?

Donald — It would be a relief.

Melania — ... but that would have other repercussions.

Donald — Whatever.

Melania — If I can't express my thoughts... I would shut down sexually.

Donald — (stopping) Pressure tactics, too? Amazing. An extremist in my own bedroom.

Melania — Ever since I've become more intellectually aware... I find it difficult to separate thought from sex. They have become fused. You know what I think it is?

Donald — (heading for the door) Could not care less.
Melania — It's a higher stage of personal development.
Donald — Fantastic. And you know what? You can have it all to yourself, because I'm fed up with you and don't give a damn anymore.

At the door, ready to exit, he looks back at her.

Melania — It's cold out. You should wear a hat.
Donald — I'm not wearing a hat!

He exits.

9

10: 30 am. The White House. Melania is standing by the window in her bedroom.

Melania — (to herself) I really like that idea of a department of race relations... start early in school... help bridge the divide... in our nation... in the world... and they could do research on motivation... so people can do more on their own... it could be called the department of MORR. MOtivation and Race Relations. I'm excited.

She crosses to the table and then back to the window.

Melania — (to herself) I told her 10:30.

Knock at the door. She goes to answer. She opens and in steps Ivanka. The two women embrace and kiss air.

Melania — I'm so glad you could come.
Ivanka — Of course. You sounded worried.
Melania — I suppose I am. Come, have a seat.

They sit at the table.

Melania — How do you like your new office?
Ivanka — I love it.
Melania — Did you ever dream of having an office in the White House?
Ivanka — Never. I shudder when I think of it. And I hope it never ends.
Melania — (dropping her eyes) That's how I feel too.
Ivanka — You look worried, Melania, what is it?
Melania — Your father.

Ivanka — What?

Melania — I didn't want to bother you but I need to talk to someone about it.

Ivanka — But what is it? Out with it, you've got me all worried too.

Melania — I think he's not… being considerate enough. I mean, as republicans, we strongly believe that people make their own luck… but there's limits to that.

Ivanka — There are…

Melania — Now that we're in a position of power we realize how much we can influence events. And it becomes clear to me that sometimes people are overwhelmed by their circumstances and they can't make their own luck.

Ivanka — True.

Melania — Even your father's base… the poor I mean, those folks have had trouble sorting things out and staying competitive…

Ivanka — I agree. Dad benefitted from noticing that. And we're here because of that alliance he made. He made it happen… he stoked their fears and galvanized them.

Melania stares at Ivanka.

Ivanka — What?

Melania — You're sounding just like him.

Ivanka — I am, aren't I?

Melania — You really believe that his hate mongering is productive?

Ivanka shakes her head slowly.

Melania — That's what I mean. He needs to stop. It's not just his attacks on immigrants and the travel suspension he's proposed, but the attack on judges, on the press. He needs to become a President.

Ivanka — He has to stop tweeting so much.

Melania — For starters.

Ivanka — I've told him already. But he's so stubborn.

Melania — Exactly. He could do a lot of good... and not just him... but all of us... with our ideas... we could help a lot of people... just because of our positions of influence.

Ivanka — I like it up here... I don't want to give it up.

Melania — And the thing is, he loves it, too.

Ivanka — You're really worried, aren't you?

Melania — Yes. Who knows how deep this Russia thing goes.

Ivanka — It's going to wash over. Dad would never have been party to anything like that. Some people around him, maybe. Those looking to take advantage of their connections. But not dad. I'm sure about that. He's red blooded all the way through.

Melania — I pray to God you're right.

Ivanka — I'm not sure about a lot of things, but I'm absolutely sure about that. Dad's a funny guy... and he loves his riches... but more than that, he loves being the star. For him, the pursuit of wealth has the ultimate objective of being the center of attention. Wealth as a means to stardom.

Melania — I think there's more to it. In his extreme views, his support of torture also... I see something deeply antidemocratic and it concerns me. We stand for something. As our President, he must negotiate with world leaders, but you don't have to praise them when you know they're autocrats or dictators.

Ivanka — It's his style.

Melania — He can't hold his tongue... it's not good judgment... it's an issue of character.

Ivanka — It worries me, too. But it may just be insecurity... he's acting like he's going to get fired any moment.

Melania — An insecurity like that, in his position... is very scary.

Ivanka — He stays so restless...

Melania — I'm trying my best.

Ivanka — I worry about his health. He told me he's getting a woman doctor. That it would help bring up his approval ratings with women and millennials. You knew about that?

Melania — Yes. And I asked him for an all-women security detail.

Ivanka — (laughs) Your Presidential escort?

Melania — Yes.

Ivanka — What a lovely idea. It's fabulous. That *would* raise his ratings.

Melania — He told me he's working on it. But please keep it to yourself.

Ivanka — Of course.

Melania gets up and walks to the window.

Ivanka — What is it, Melania?

She rises and follows her.

Melania — I'm not getting through. He wants me to just agree with him but I can't do that. He goes on about my wifely duties as first lady and just wanting to relax when he's with me. Do you get Jared his slippers?

Ivanka — Jared doesn't do slippers. But I get him other things. Of course, he reciprocates.

Melania — And I do get him the slippers, but...

Ivanka — Melania... before the White House... had you guys had an ongoing discussion of ideas?

Melania — No. I would bring up an issue now and then but I wouldn't pursue it.

Ivanka — So this is all pretty new to him, your being vocal with your ideas?

Melania — Yes. It's my fault. I should've been more courageous. And I was with other subjects, he knows that... but I wasn't political. I stayed away from the subject.

Ivanka — And then the campaign happened.

Melania — Yes. Seeing so many people voicing their thoughts... and being so forceful about it... made a deep impression on me. And then, suddenly—I never really expected it to happen—we're in the White House.

Ivanka — It was a surprise to all of us.

Melania — It may have seemed to him like an abrupt change on my part... but it had been brewing for the longest.

Ivanka — And now he has this new reality to adapt to.

Melania — Yes.
Ivanka turns and walks back to the table and sits. Melania follows.

Melania — Can I get you anything to drink?
Ivanka — No, thanks. No one said any of this would be easy, for any of us. We're all under the microscope. Everybody is. And for all his love of the limelight... he's tense and afraid to fail... let himself and all of us down.
Melania — We've talked about that. His fear of failing in front of the whole world. I've talked to him about doing only one term.
Ivanka — What?
Melania — To ease the pressure on him.
Ivanka — (shaking her head) I disagree. There's no turning back once you get to this point. There's only one way to go and it's forward. He'll adapt.
Melania — I don't think it's good for him. The more stress the more impulsive.
Ivanka — We just need to keep talking to him—being the opposition in a way—the opposition right in his innermost circle.
Melania — (to herself, doubtfully) No rest for the weary.
Ivanka — We must move forward... we all like it in here.

They look at each other for a moment.

Melania — But, even as I've asked him to do only one term... I'd want it to be the best it could possibly be.
Ivanka — Two terms would be better than one. I'm barely spreading my wings. Do you have a specific plan, to get him to be less impulsive?
Melania — I've thought of shocking him.
Ivanka — Now wait, you don't mean electrically?
Melania — Of course not, silly.
Ivanka — Then what?
Melania — You have to promise you won't share it with anyone.
Ivanka — I promise.
Melania — I thought of converting to Islam.

Ivanka doesn't believe her ears.

Ivanka — I didn't hear that. You mean, changing your faith?
Melania — Yes.
Ivanka — Oh my God, Melania, you've gone nuts! That's the craziest thing I've ever heard. You do something like that and he'll have a heart attack. Please, don't do that. You'll kill him. He's my father! I wouldn't do that to your dad.
Melania — I would bring it up slowly, in increments.
Ivanka — How in increments?
Melania — I would start reading the Quran and telling him about it.
Ivanka — He would go bonkers, I know he would.
Melania — He won't. I've already brought it up.
Ivanka — What did he say, how did he react?
Melania — He had a fit but then begged me not to do it.

Ivanka leans forward, arms on her knees, shaking her head.

Ivanka — There has to be another way...
Melania — And as I build up momentum... I would be insinuating the possibility of going public.
Ivanka — What? Melania, it would be a national scandal. Worse than if you had an affair. Why are you telling me all of this?
Melania — Because I need your help.
Ivanka — Help you convert to Islam? Melania, I'm Jewish. I already converted. Once is enough!
Melania — Ivanka... all you would need to do is tell him that you think I'm serious.
Ivanka — (suddenly relieved) You're not?
Melania — Of course I am, but deep down he thinks I'm just trying to manipulate him.
Ivanka — Wait a second, isn't that what this is?
Melania — No.
Ivanka — Oh my god. For a moment I thought that's what you were trying to do.
Melania — It started that way. But the more I think of it, the more I realize that if I convert I would be making an important

contribution to world peace. Imagine the newspaper headings, the world over, 'American First Lady Embraces Islam'.

Ivanka — Melania, you have lost your marbles. You can't rush history. It needs to take its time.

Melania — I'm in a position to influence world affairs.

Ivanka — Melania, darling, the first lady thing has gone to your head.

Melania — You don't think I should have a voice?

Ivanka — You're not just wanting a voice, you're wanting a loudspeaker. You were not elected to the office.

Melania — I will not be just an ornament.

Ivanka — I didn't mean it that way.

Melania — And I do not intend to waste the power of the office, either. Imagine the headline, 'Muslim First Lady and Jewish Daughter on First Trip to Middle East'.

Ivanka cracks up with laughter.

Ivanka — (still laughing)- 'President vows not to deport wife'.

Melania smiles.

Ivanka — (suddenly worried again) We're not being recorded, are we?

Melania — Not that I know of, I hope not.

Ivanka — I wonder if Nixon taped his bedroom conversations.

Melania — We would've known by now.

Ivanka — True.

Ivanka seems to relax a little, then starts laughing again.

Melania — I need to get some nice scarves that I can fashion into hijabs.

Ivanka — Some are very pretty and colorful.

Melania — I've noticed.

Ivanka looks at Melania.

Ivanka — What we will do for love...

Melania — That's very true.

Ivanka — (worried) You're not planning to go anywhere with the hijab, are you?

Melania — Of course not.

Ivanka — Have you started reading the Quran?

Melania — Yes. I found a copy in the presidential library. So nobody knows. You think his base would forgive him if I converted?

Ivanka — It's a love affair between those two but... that's a tough one. I don't know.

Ivanka sits back, smooths her long hair, the expression thoughtful.

Ivanka — You know that the Muslim bashing was tactical.

Melania — Tactical?

Ivanka — Yes. Simply to get elected.

Melania — Doesn't that scare you, that he would do that? Stir up all that rage? Who knows how many people have been hurt because of it?

Ivanka — His writers are already at work on the speech that he will give to the Saudis when he visits... probably in May.

Melania — How will he handle that?

Ivanka — He'll focus on the fight against ISIS. We talked about it.

Melania — He thinks everything is negotiable... even democracy.

Ivanka — I wouldn't go that far.

Melania — Would a believer in democracy be in favor of waterboarding?

Ivanka — That was weird. I disagree with him. But he's said he'll defer to Jim on that and Jim's not in favor.

They look at each other in silence.

Melania — I have often told him that he can be a good President, not just an impulsive showman... but I don't know anymore.

Ivanka — We're all under quite a bit of stress. Speaking of which... I have to get back.

Melania — Of course.

Ivanka — We need to do this again.
Melania — We must.

They get up, embrace, kiss air, and Ivanka strides to the door.

Ivanka — (turning back at the door) I'm glad you've finally found your voice.
Melania — It took a while.
Ivanka — And it will be good for you and for him. Bye now.
Melania — Bye.

10

It's the middle of the day and Donald is in his bedroom—sitting at the table—by himself.

He picks up the phone and tweets—3/9/17 — We are making great progress with healthcare. ObamaCare is imploding and will only get worse. Republicans coming together to get job done!

He puts the phone down.

Donald — I needed to get away for a bit. Be alone with my thoughts. Reince is the only one who knows where I am. He'll come get me if he needs to. There's so much going on in my mind... I need a little privacy.
(he rubs his face, clasps his hands and stretches up his arms, a good long stretch. He feels the tension slowly ease out of him and he smiles, pleased with himself)

Look at me. Kid from New York makes good. I wish dad were here, he'd be so proud of what I've done. And mom. The other night they came to me in my sleep. I rarely dream but it's happening more often... they just stood there, glowing with satisfaction. And I said, 'Hey pops, not a bad return on that million dollars you gave me to get started, don't you think?' And he says, 'I knew you had it in you.' Strong stuff. It was a nice visit. I wouldn't mind if they came back now and then.
(he gets up and walks to the window. He throws open the drapes and the sunlight streams into the room)

What a feeling. Becoming immortal. Kid from New York who started out in real estate. And here I am, President of the United States. Amazing. To be sure... it's a bit stressful at times but... I just can't let it get to me.

(he shakes his head slowly, an expression of wonderment surfacing)

Wow... what a story... my rise to power. One day I'll see it on the screen. The whole nation will be there, too... mesmerized... on the edge of their seats... and the ratings will be fantastic... I can see the title already... TRUMP... and I'll make Hollywood beg for the rights. How can it not happen... I'm such a tragic figure... (he stops, suddenly a worried look) did I say tragic? Hmm. I did, didn't I? Was that my unconscious slipping in something for me to look at? Goddammit! All this talking with Melania is starting to give me the creeps. Forget her. I need to get away.
(he paces the room)

At first I thought I couldn't do it... but then I got into that first debate and just improvised... no notes... just winged it and held my own... surprised the heck out of myself, carrying on as I was... in front of the whole world... and I couldn't believe the moderator didn't stop and tell me, 'You're fired! Leave the stage!'
(he stops, laughs)

I was getting away with doing my thing and pushing past all these supposedly seasoned politicians. I even told Jeb Bush to shut it up. And he did. On national TV. You never know what you can get away with until you try.
(he crosses to the window and shouts out)

I am the 45th President of the United States of America! And I'm ready for it, so bring it on, goddammit!
(laughing loudly)

When I think of all the things I had to do to get here. That's the movie right there. I wonder who could play me? Definitely not that obnoxious guy with the wig on Saturday Night Live. I can't even remember his name.
(the mood now pensive)

Boy, the advances for my memoirs will be huge... and my presidential library will be in New York... and I should ask Frank Gehry to start working on the design... and there will be a whole wing devoted to my tweet collection... where scholars will pore over my thoughts... wow... just took it away from Hillary, didn't I? She knew her stuff, though, stood her ground, looked Presidential, whereas I was always just playing off of her. I'm sure she won those debates but, by then, I had done such a masterful job of devaluing her that it didn't matter that she knew more than I did. She wouldn't have been a bad President, either. And she would've done all right by my base, the poor side of it. But heck, I beat her to the punch. And that wonderful line, 'put her in jail!' Loved that one. It caught on nicely and riled the folks.
(the mood now worried)

When is Melania going to get over it? It's not that we don't have our sweet moments... I just hate the mouth she's got. She always had a mouth, though, and I kind of liked it... but now it's ten times worse. Maybe if I give in on the idea of an all-female Presidential escort. I know she wants it but the secret service is pushing back. I'm going to keep working on it. I'd score some points with women libbers which wouldn't hurt. Not with millennials, though. Those kids hate my guts. But if she goes ahead with the Muslim thing I'm going to have a meltdown and it won't be pretty. I might even divorce her. Even though I love that woman. But I've been down that road before.
(smiling again)

I like fresh starts. New beginnings. It's been a while since there was a single man as President.
Hmm. If Angela was not married I'd go for her. Kinda cute, too. Now that would be intercontinental dating for you. I'd go over one weekend, she'd come over the next. Beautiful. And the press would love it. My ratings would soar. But she's married... oh well... I'd have to look elsewhere... China's a possibility... never had a Chinese girlfriend... would do wonders for the relationship between our two countries. Might even have a baby with her. Hmm. China then would

get serious about putting pressure on Kim in North Korea to ease up on the missile threat. Hmm. No telling what a little loving can do.
(he walks to the window)

More people running for President should be single... marry leaders in other nations and help world peace. With the speed of modern travel... getting together wouldn't be a problem. Food for thought. When Ivanka becomes president... hmm... of course, she'd have to dump Jared first. But I'm getting ahead of myself.
(he is clearly enjoying this moment alone)

God, how I love my base. Both the rich *and* the poor in my base. And what I love the most is that they understand me. I can feel it and see it in their faces... and they love me because I'm one of them. It's a love fest, all right. How can you beat that?
(he pauses)

Now... did my love for my base come before I thought of running for President... or after? There's that Melania getting into my head again. Hmm. To be really honest... the love for my base didn't heat up until I decided to run. But heck, I was busy building my empire. They'll forgive me.
(fingers laced he puts his hands over his head)

I just hope my people are patient with me... I do worry they don't get that. If I'm being a bit rash with my executive orders and my proposals, it's just me trying to please. As for the folks who think I'm in it for the money, they're dead wrong. I've got money. I'm set. I've been set for the longest. God knows I ran over enough people to get where I am. But that's life. Ruthless. Cruel sometimes.
(he takes a boxing stance, does a little shuffle and throws a couple of punches in the air)

And if you want to be a true American, brother, you've got to love competition. And know also, that competition is a blood sport and you can get hurt,
(he throws another two punches)

and if you don't like it, get out of the way. We'll send you a social
security check and a bag of potato chips so you can watch from
the stands.
(opening his arms widely)

Baby, I've got what it takes! And I've proved it again and again!
Look at all I've built.
(he smiles proudly)

That's why I never get depressed. The moment I've just an inkling
of it, I look out the window and there's another Trump Tower. My
adrenaline goes right back up. Why? Because I have the tenacity
and the work ethic and the drive, and to all those people who
love to bad mouth me I say, look at yourselves in the mirror and
recognize that you're just envious. Own up to it. Be a man. Or a
Woman. Whatever.
(he lowers his head, pensively now)

I wonder what it would be like to be a regular person. Average
drive, average energy, average inventiveness, settling for anything.
It's scary. Hmmm. It's so scary I'd be running all day long just to get
away from myself. Is that why people use drugs? Hmm. But that's
just too much introspection. My thing is the pursuit of glory. The
relentless quest to accomplish. That's what sets me apart.
(pausing, serious mood)

I'd really like to be a good President, though. But it does occur
to me, now and then, that maybe I'm not cut out for it. Not
that I'd ever say that to anyone. Not even Melania. But I may
be more cut out to being a billionaire. Mercurial. Extravagant.
Loud. Opinionated. But then again... I could be all that and still be
President.

Knock at the door. He crosses to it but doesn't open.

Reince — Mr. President?
Donald — Reince?

Reince — Yes, Mr. President. Sir, when you get a moment, we need you at the Oval Office.
Donald — Can it wait a little while?
Reince — Of course. Can you join us in 20 minutes?
Donald — I'll be there. Thank you.
Reince — You're welcome Mr. President.

Reince leaves.

Donald — I love being called Mr. President.
(he returns to the window)
The one drawback I have... and I know I have to work on it... is that I'm not a consensus builder. I recognize that. And I worry that it may be my undoing... not being able to bring the country together... but maybe the talks with Melania will help correct it. It's just that... well... it's not me... it feels forced... fake... I love shoving people out of my way... firing them... right and left... you're out of here!
(he laughs)

I know it won't be easy...
(he goes to the table and sits)

Talking about firing... the FBI guy may be next. Fellow trying to make a name for himself. Commendable. But not at my expense. When he brought up Hillary's private emails with just 11 days to the election, I knew he was dangerous. It worked for me but I knew, right then, he could turn around and stick it to me, too. And it's not like I didn't try to win him over. I offered him my friendship but he wasn't interested. He had to be independent. Okay. Have it your way, buster. I've read enough about old J. Edgar Hoover, how he had it in for Kennedy. Yep... just waiting... and it's gonna be a splash, too. You're fired! Outta here! I can see the headlines.
(he laughs)

Anyway, I need to fire someone now and then, just to keep them on their toes. There's Murhpy's law, but there's Trump's law, too...

if you can do it, do it! Wow, I keep getting all these ideas... but back to the consensus builder thing... not easy. The thing is... to be a consensus builder... to be a President for all Americans... I'd have to learn to think like regular folks... understand their limitations... accept that they don't have these gifts that I possess... hmm... but wouldn't that be making excuses for people... wouldn't that be thinking like a democrat?
(leaning forward, he clasps his hands, the mood serious)

Come to think of it... a lot of the people who helped me get so rich were regular folks. I couldn't have done it without them. And they had their limitations... but still they helped me become who I am. They believed in me. Hmm. I could be more thoughtful.
(getting up, he straightens up his tie, then steps over to the mirror, looks at himself, pats his hair down)

The mane of a Viking. A warrior. But enough of this. I'd better get back to the Oval Office. The world misses me. What a feeling. I'll have to do this again some other time. I wish I would have taped myself...
(still looking at himself, he arranges a strand of unruly hair)

Better not. Nixon did that and look what happened to him.
(he winks at himself in the mirror)

Which reminds me... on that speech to the Saudis, for when I visit in May... I can say Islam is a great religion... I can say that... nothing wrong with that... heck, I'll say anything to get the deal... fact is I had to do some Muslim bashing to get elected and that's that. And if I have to do it all over again, so be it. Come to think of it, I can whip that sucker all the way to the next election. The Saudis will understand. They're strong men like me. Imposing our will on the people. You're doing good, Donald, doing good, boy. Now back to the limelight.

He strides to the door and exits.

On 3/24/17, Not having enough support to pass, the
republican party withdrew the American Health Care
Act bill before putting it to a vote in the House.
Conservatives (Freedom Caucus) argued that the
law looked too much like Obamacare. This, despite
concessions from proponents to remove federal
mandates that covered maternity and mental health
care.

The proposed law included deep cuts to the Medicaid
program. The Congressional Budget Office (non
partisan) estimated that passage would lead to 24
million fewer Americans having health insurance
over the next 10 years.

3/24 — Trump tweets—The irony is that the Freedom
Caucus, which is very pro-life and against Planned
Parenthood, allows P.P. to continue if they stop
this plan.

3/24 — Trump said, "We learned a lot about loyalty,
and we learned a lot about the vote-getting
process... certainly for me, it was a very interesting experience."

11

Donald is sitting quietly at the table, the expression glum, eyes fixed on his phone but not tweeting. Melania is standing by the window looking back at him.

Melania — It's not the end of the world.
Donald — I tried to make light of it with the press but it's killing me inside.
Melania — You have to put up with the pain.
Donald — (turning to her) Is that the comfort you're going to offer?
Melania — Yes. Hold your pain, don't tweet it off.
Donald — (irritated) Don't treat me like a child! I am the President of the United States.

He puts the phone down.

Donald — I tried to negotiate with the right but they would have none of it. I gave it my best. They're a stubborn bunch.
Melania — And they're not going away either.
Donald — We'll have to figure out a strategy.

He gets up and joins her by the window.

Melania — They're part of the swamp you kept talking about.
Donald — They're not the core of my base.
Melania — So then, they can be left out.
Donald — (looking at her) I needed their votes. Anyway, weren't you pushing for me to be President for all Americans? You need to make up your mind.
Melania — Good point.
Donald — Everybody's making a big deal about this setback. The legendary deal maker didn't come through. But that's not how

I see it. I have to learn some things and it's going to take longer than I thought.

Melania — Humbling.

Donald — I've been there before.

Melania — You didn't know much about health care, did you?

Donald — I didn't. And neither did the people that put forward the plan. That's what bugs me the most.

She takes a step back and crosses her arms.

Melania — But that didn't keep you from carrying on and on about Obamacare being this horrible program.

Donald — The press is right... for once. We had been slinging mud at Obamacare for seven years but didn't bother to draw up a solid alternative. And the party let me down because they hadn't done their homework. I didn't have to be in such a rush...

Melania — What's wrong with the individual mandate, asking everyone to pay for health insurance?

Donald — It's a tax.

Melania — Isn't it the responsible thing to do, for everybody, young or old, to pay for insurance to dilute the cost to the sick?

Donald — I'm not adding taxes. That's Obama.

Melania — The young will get old one day... why shouldn't they help share the burden, and be penalized if they don't?

Donald — Melania... there's a time and an obligation to make money. A time and an obligation to plan ahead and provide for yourself in old age. That's life. That's being responsible.

Melania — And if you didn't do it, or simply could not, then you're out of luck?

Donald — The safety net is meant to soften the blow. But only a little. Otherwise we corrupt the values that have made us great. Self-reliance. Hard work. You reap what you sow.

Melania — I've read that the Swiss, the Germans, Singapore also, manage to provide universal coverage without the single payer system. We could learn from them.

Donald — We're different.

Melania — And they do it by having everybody pitch in, but not just that, being believers in free markets they have many insurance companies so there's greater competition. Why can't we have that here, too? Are we not the party of competition?

Donald — There's been mergers... and there's been acquisitions... and big companies swallow the little ones.

Melania — And we end up with oligopolies.

Donald — Big fish eats little fish.

Melania — The big fish who have access to politicians who need their money to get elected, and then those politicians doing what the big fish want.

Donald — Survival of the fittest.

Melania — The big fish and the politicians, conveniently forgetting that, next to individual responsibility, there's social responsibility, and the one being as important as the other.

Donald — There you go, revving up again...

Melania — And it's that social responsibility—the notion of the public good—that your base... I should correct myself... the *poor* in your base, wanted you to stand up for because they had missed out on it. Because if there had been that public concern in the first place, the *poor* in your base wouldn't be where they are, instead they would've taken advantage of training programs and they would've had hope...

Donald — I got that!

Melania — ...and their communities would not have taken a hit with the economic changes, or been ravaged by the opioid epidemic... but there you were ready to push a bill that would've benefitted mostly the employers... saving them money but harming your base because Medicaid would have been cut, or their premiums and out of pocket expenses would have gone up.

He looks off, silently.

Donald — The right wing wanted the bill to reflect more emphasis on personal responsibility...

She takes a step toward the window and gazes out for a moment.

Melania — And you couldn't stand up to them.

Donald — I tried to. In fact, I wanted revenge... but then I talked to Paul. It's complicated.

Melania — Is it? Doesn't everyone start out wanting to do well, Dee, everyone... and then things happen... and some become irresponsible or morally reprehensible... but they're still people...

Donald — You missed your calling, dear, you should've gone into social work.

Melania — ... which happens to be exactly one of the things the nation needs... so we can connect better with each other, gifted with the less gifted, rich with poor, black with white... and strengthen our foundation.

He returns to the table and sits. He rubs his face slowly, the mood dejected but fighting it.

Donald — Melania... I am a politician. I am a deal maker. To get things done I have to negotiate, to deal with the world as it is. It will take a little time before I deliver to my base... but deliver I will because with the tax cuts that are on the way... there will be the big, huge, never seen before infrastructure projects, so everybody who wants to work will get to work... and then they will have enough money to pay for the increased premiums and what they need...

Melania — Really, Dee?

Donald — ... and it will raise the living standards of my people... and we will be great again!

Melania — And the big companies, the contractors, the already advantaged, will make lots of money, and sure, the workers will get something, too, and maybe they'll have enough for the increased premiums and a few extra things... but the differential will stay the same.

Donald — The differential?

Melania — The gap between the rich and the poor will not narrow. And if it doesn't narrow there will not be enough to go around.

Donald — Rewards should be limitless, Melania... that is a key republican concept... limitless rewards... for the creator, for the enterprising, for the daring. The democrats want to undermine that. I say to you I can still lift the poor in my base while preserving the rewards for the gifted.

Melania — Did you tell them that during the campaign?

Donald — It's a subtle point.

Melania — It's a central point. And because you hold it dear, you will not be able to deliver on your promises to the poor in your base.

Donald — There you go again... 'Melania, the Great Seer'. Have you not heard of the trickle-down effect? Or have you not got to that chapter yet?

She looks at him for a moment, then crosses to her closet and pulls out a coat.

Donald — Where are you going?

Melania — For a walk.

She walks to the door and opens it to exit.

Melania — Oh, I meant to tell you. I saw two comparison photos of the Los Angeles' sky. The one from 1973 had the entire downtown covered in smog. The one from this year was very clear. The difference was striking.

Donald — My base is not in LA.

Melania — They're Americans, too.

Donald — I know coal is on the way out... but it's going to be slow.

She is about to exit...

Donald — It's cold outside... wear a hat.

Melania — I don't need a hat!

And she walks out.

Donald — (to himself) No cuchi cuchi tonight.

3/26/17n — Trump tweets—Democrats are smiling in
D.C. that the Freedom Caucus, with the help of
Club For Growth and Heritage, have saved Planned
Parenthood and Ocare!

3/26 — And he tweets—General Kelly is doing a great
job at the border. Numbers are way down. Many are
not even trying to come in anymore.

12

Donald is sitting at the table looking at the news in his phone. She is by the window.

Donald — Unbelievable...
Melania — What?
Donald — The attack on Westminster bridge in London... the Islamic State claimed responsibility... three people killed... forty injured...
Melania — Very sad. You wonder when this madness is going to end.
Donald — Do you understand now why I want the travel restriction?
Melania — The security measures we have in place are protecting us.
Donald — We need more. I still don't understand what's got into the Brits, electing a Muslim mayor in London.
Melania — They're a multicultural city.
Donald — They had the right idea with Brexit. Secure the borders. Hold up on the melting pot.
Melania — That's going to cost them.
Donald — The French are headed in the same direction.
Melania — Someone said that the French are contrarian, so maybe not.

She is silent for a moment.

Melania — I've been reading...
Donald — What? (a bit exasperated but still glued to his phone) Why?
Melania — It's part of my job as the first lady of the nation.
Donald — Tell me where it says that.
Melania — You don't want me to read?
Donald — That's not what I meant. I had a stressful day and what I really need is peace and quiet so I can be rested for another hectic day tomorrow... is that too much to ask?

Melania — Do you want your slippers?
Donald — Sure… that would be very nice.

She goes into his closet, fetches the slippers and puts them at his feet. He returns to his phone and she to the window.

Donald — You want some French fries?
Melania — No, thanks. It's too late. Plus you had a full dinner just three hours ago.
Donald — I'm hungry again.
Melania — You're not hungry, you're anxious.
Donald — Excuse me, I happen to know the difference. Please call the kitchen and ask them to bring me a serving of fries.
Melania — It's 11 o'clock.
Donald — So?
Melania — They're probably asleep.
Donald — I have a craving for fries, so please call the kitchen.
Melania — Call them yourself. I'm sure they'll love to hear from you.
Donald — (slamming the phone on the table) What's the problem?

He stares at her but she ignores him. Slowly, he regains his calm.

Donald — I'm sorry. (turning to her) What have you been reading?
Melania — At MIT, more than 40% of the faculty and graduate students were born outside of the country…
Donald — So?
Melania — There's a lot of science and technology applications coming out of there…
Donald — And?
Melania — We need foreigners.
Donald — Melania, I am not against foreigners… unless they break the rules.
Melania — We need foreigners to keep us on the cutting edge… to keep us innovating. It is not an option… we need the outside stimulus… we need openness… foreigners… that we can transform into Americans.

Donald — We need *talented* foreigners... which is why I'm willing to look at the Canadian immigration model... which is based on merit, not family ties like our system is.

Melania — Talented people have families, too.

Donald — Close family, that's it, no more. And follow the rules.

Melania — The people whose travel you have wanted to suspend had been following the rules...

Donald — I need to make sure... and I owe it to my people.

Melania — It was unnecessary.

Donald — Dammit! I did it because I promised my people I would do it and that's that. Call it political expedience if you'd like. The point is that it's in my power to do so.

Melania — To pander to your base... to the nativist.

Donald — I'm President and I say it's for our security, and if I have to take it all the way up to the Supreme Court, I will. Case closed.

Melania — I think you're afraid of multiculturalism...

Donald — Afraid?

Melania — And you have no idea on how to address it. You should be thinking of ways to manage the friction that newcomers create... not take advantage of it.

He gets up and joins her by the window.

Donald — 'Give me your tired, your poor, your huddled masses yearning to breathe free...' said Emma Lazarus.

Melania — '...the wretched refuse of your teeming shore...'

Donald — Beautiful words... when did she write them... 1883?

Melania — I think so.

Donald — There was no Islamic State back then. This is my world and I will do what I must.

She is quiet for a moment.

Melania — I think the campaign... and now the presidency, has brought out the worst in you.

Donald — No matter what they throw at me, I'm still standing.

Melania — You've said you've had a hard time dealing with the way I've changed... I've had a hard time dealing with the way *you've* changed. And I don't think it's good for us.

She looks up at him.

Melania — Is it worth it?
Donald — We'll get through.
Melania — That doesn't answer my question.
Donald — Look, it's not easy to get the nativist to accept that immigrants enrich the nation and improve his life. Pride gets in the way. 'You're coming here because of what we have,' the nativist tells the newcomer... 'you want a part of it... but I don't know if what you offer will be worth my troubles.' It's simpler at MIT, or other universities, where they can see the scientific papers and the evidence for accomplishment is clear. But regular folk don't see that. Regular folk don't see the gifted foreign engineer or researcher or entrepreneur... they're far removed from him or her... what they see instead is that the newcomer is as average as they are... except that he will be hungrier... more ambitious... more tenacious... or works for less... for longer hours... and that's what gets the nativist. And rather than confront that in himself... he picks on the surface differences... the accent... the skin color... the different faith... to dismiss the immigrant or put him down. And if on top of that, we ask the nativist to make room for the newcomer, to share with the immigrant, then it's all bad.
Melania — That argument is rational... but you didn't use it during the campaign.
Donald — My base needed an easy answer, not a hard one.
Melania — That's what I'm having trouble with. The choices you've made.
Donald — I needed to get in.
Melania — Under the irascible, charming, impulsive showman's façade, lies a cunning that is disturbing.
Donald — I've needed every bit of it to get to where I am ... I couldn't've built an empire without it. But I'm glad you see that part of me.

Melania — I don't like it.
Donald — It's who I am.

They are quiet for a moment, side by side.

Donald — It's a rough patch we're going through… that's all.
Melania — I want to believe that.
Donald — It's all it is, a rough patch. Things will settle down.

He takes her hand in his.

Donald — I meant to tell you… the FBI guy called up today and said I was not under investigation.
Melania — Feeling relieved?
Donald — I don't know what to believe from this guy. Except that he wants to keep his job.

They both remain standing next to each other as they gaze out into the D.C. night.

Melania — Did you ask any of your associates to get Russia to meddle in the election?
Donald — (takes a moment to answer) It feels strange having you ask me that question. It says something about the erosion of trust between us.
Melania — It does.
Donald — Maybe we *are* becoming strangers to each other.
Melania — It is sad. Will you answer my question, please?
Donald — I never asked any of my associates to get Russia to meddle in the election.
Melania — Thank you.
Donald — Does that satisfy you?
Melania — It does.

They're silent for a moment.

Donald — It's all about difference, isn't it? About uniqueness... rewarding drive and accomplishment... otherwise we'll have nothing.

Melania — The less able have a dignity that needs to be respected.

Donald — You have to make an effort... to put yourself out... be responsible.

Melania — Some people have trouble with that and need help.

Donald — Add to welfare? Set up a universal basic income?

Melania — Why not offering help to free up the drive to create? We all have it. For one reason or another, it gets bottled up in some people.

Donald — Send a fleet of mental health people to every distressed community?

Melania — That would be a wonderful first step. Would you do that during your term?

Donald — The party wouldn't dream of it.

Melania — Ah, the party. We're too quick to judge that those in need are not worthy... But we all have value... every one of us... and we're all insecure (she turns to him) Aren't you insecure?

Donald — I suppose. A little.

Melania — A lot.

Donald — Why, thanks.

Melania — And so am I. Enter the quick moral judgment to keep us safe... to make us feel better than our brothers and sisters... to help us protect our advantage...

Donald — Melania, to thrive we have to compete. That's the world we live in... and when we find an advantage we make the most of it... not sure of how long it will last, which is what I did.

Melania — You had a cool million to get you going.

Donald — (smiling) True.

Melania — During his campaign, at one of his rallies, in France, Macron was asked by a man in the audience, why couldn't he have a suit like the one Macron was wearing? And he answered he would have to work for it. The man said he was working two jobs already and still couldn't afford it. I don't know what Macron replied in turn but the question laid out the issue.

Donald — That man has choices to make, and maybe live without the suit.

Melania — But does the man have a fair playing field, does he have opportunity? That's what the question is.

Donald — And if he applies himself and still can't get the suit, will he remain engaged and not give up and live in resentment?

Melania — That's part of dialogue we should be having.

Donald — And you don't think I'm doing that?

Melania — You're not even thinking about it.

They pause.

Donald — There's a lot on my plate. I thought it would be easier... this being President. But I've told you that, already.

Melania — I'm your wife. I get to hear you repeat yourself.

Donald — It would help if I could score some points... the health care bill not passing is still bugging me...

Melania — Try working with the democrats... that's more than half the votes you got.

Donald — Don't rub it in.

Melania — You carried on like we were supposed to expect miracles from you once you took office.

Donald — True.

Melania — First day in office you would declare China a currency manipulator... and all kinds of jobs would materialize.

Donald — I did say that, didn't I? I'm sure it got me some votes. What do you think of Xi?

Melania — He wants to be emperor.

Donald — We'll meet them soon. I'm envious.

Melania — Isn't being President good enough?

Donald — Let's say it's my insecurity. But the press is not helping. (he puts his arm around her)
Earlier today, a journalist tweeted that my choices are showing I'm shortsighted. But if so, I've built an empire being short sighted. If so, I won an election that nobody thought I could win. (and turning to look at her)

If so, I spotted you out of the crowd and married you. So, hallelujah for shortsightedness.
Melania — Did you tweet that?
Donald — No, that's private.
Melania — (drawing closer and circling his wait with her arm) Thank you for the compliment.
Donald — You're welcome.

They pause.

Donald — Do you want a glass of cider?
Melania — I'd like that.

He takes her by the hand and they walk back to the table.

Donald — Let me call for a bottle.
Melania — Never mind. I keep one in the closet, so we don't have to bother them in the middle of the night.
Donald — What do you think about Ivanka getting her own office?
Melania — It's great having her close by.

She goes into her closet and pulls out the unopened bottle of cider and a bag of crackers. There are two glasses on the table. She hands him the crackers and proceeds to open the bottle.

Melania — The crackers are low fat.
Donald — (tastes one) Mmm... delicious.
Melania — Oh, just got myself some pretty scarves.
Donald — You have scarves.
Melania — These are special. I'll show them to you another day.
Donald — You think we can keep growing the Trump brand while we're in the White House? I mean, it's always good to have a backup plan.
Melania — Yes... and the better job you do as President, the more it will grow, without having to do anything else. I mean, doubling the membership at Mar-a-Lago right after you won the election was not necessary. In fact, it was self serving.

Donald — I suppose so. It's done. But we won't make any further increases. Or maybe just to keep up with inflation.

He pours the cider and they toast.

Donald — To power.
Melania — To good deeds.
Donald — To America first.
Melania — To mankind.

They sip from their glasses.

Donald — We didn't quite agree on the toast, did we?
Melania — Variety is the spice of life.
Donald — You think the toast counted?
Melania — Sure it did. A toast is a toast.
Donald — (raising his glass again)—To us!
Melania — To you and me!

They drink again.

Donald — Can't you just repeat what I say?
Melania — What's the big deal?
Donald — It would mean a lot to me.
Melania — Okay. If it means that much to you.
Donald — (raising his glass again) To love!
Melania — (she looks him in the eye for a moment... then softly) To love.

They clink and drink.

Donald — You don't like my slogan, America First, do you?
Melania — It would make sense as a rallying cry if you were calling for us to give our collective best... but the way you deliver it is divisive, as if saying, 'we—as in some of us—are the best... we have been the best and will be the best'... and while we're at it we wouldn't mind if the rest of the folks went down on one knee.

But in an era of era of ever increasing international cooperation, where we've benefitted and stand to benefit as much as others have, it comes across as shallow and provincial.
Donald — Not exceptional?

She shakes her head.

Melania — We've had exceptional moments... but we killed each other over the right to enslave a man... and held on to Jim Crow for nearly a century after. Not that we could not still become an exceptional people... but it's a work in progress.

He hangs his head for a moment.

Donald — Want to go for a walk?
Melania — This late?
Donald — Heck, why not?
Melania — In your robe?
Donald — In my robe.
Melania — It's chilly.
Donald — Let's do it!

They rise and exit.

3/27/17 — Trump tweets—The Democrats will make a
deal with me on healthcare as soon as ObamaCare
folds—not long. Do not worry, we are in very good
shape.

Medicaid, signed into law in 1965 by Lyndon
Johnson, now covers 74 million people.

3/28 — Trump tweets—The failing @NYTimes would do
much better if they were honest.

3/28 — Trump signs order to undo Obama's Clean
Power Plan, which aimed to reduce greenhouse gas
emissions by lowering coal production. The U.S. is
the world's second largest carbon dioxide producer,
behind China and ahead of India.

Gallup Daily: Trump Job Approval—56% disapprove
while 36% approve.

The nation still waits for Trump's tax returns.

13

It's the middle of the day and Donald comes into their bedroom.

Donald — Melania? Sweetheart?

No reply. The bathroom door is ajar.

Donald — You in there?

No reply. He crosses to the window and stands there a moment, looking out. Now Melania steps out of the bathroom. She has covered her head and most of her face with a pretty scarf, in the style of a hijab. When he turns and sees her he is aghast.

Donald — What is that?
Melania — A scarf... arranged into a hijab.
Donald — Could you please remove it?
Melania — No, I want to wear it for a while.

He crosses to the table and sits down. She sits too.

Donald — Let's be clear about this... you do not want to convert to Islam, do you?
Melania — I have no immediate plans.
Donald — What does that mean?
Melania — Just that. I may decide to do it later.
Donald — If you do... you realize you would be destroying my presidency?
Melania — If I did... I would be humanizing your presidency.
Donald — You obviously have not thought this through. Have you talked to anyone about it?
Melania — I spoke to Ivanka.
Donald — My own daughter.

Melania — I told her to keep it between us.
Donald — She probably told Jared already, and who knows whom he spoke to.
Melania — I'm sure Ivanka kept it to herself. Look, I am on your side, I do not want to harm you.
Donald — Is that so? What do you think my base will think?
Melania — I don't know. But it may give them pause, and help them review their convictions.

Leaning forward, he drops his face in his hands.

Melania — Dee...
Donald — And I had brought good news to you.
Melania — What?
Donald — What do you care?
Melania — What's the good news?
Donald — The secret service will give you an all women Presidential escort. They'll have to set it up.
Melania — Thank you. That is beautiful, really is.
Donald — And this is how you repay me?
Melania — Dee... I am not converting to Islam.
Donald — You're not?
Melania — No. I'm simply trying to get familiar with it.
Donald — What if you let one of the maids in and she sees you wearing it? She'll call the New York Times right away. Or the Washington Post. Or the LA Times, the Atlantic, the Guardian, you name it, any of the vile rags that are making my life miserable. I will be surprised if they don't have paid informers here in the White House, and it could be one of the maids, the butler, your dentist.
Melania — Please let me finish?

He shakes his head disconsolately.

Melania — I am the first lady of the country. I have an obligation to help lead.
Donald — Where in the constitution does it say that?

Melania — It's implicit... that as your wife I should do my best to keep you doing the right thing.

Donald — (growing exasperated) I am doing the right thing, it takes time to get the deals!

Melania — You're not building bridges... we're as divided as just after the election, or even more so... there's no inclination on your part...

Donald — So how does your converting to Islam going to help things?

Melania — I told you I'm not converting... but I'd like to bring Islam into our home... so it can help you see Muslims as people... not devils... but people like you and me.

Donald — (standing up) Of course they're people like you and me. They're great people, too. But I needed to get elected, didn't I? And I didn't have time to waste. I have no personal animosity toward Muslims. I'm dealing with Arab leaders all the time. Now that I'm President I have to negotiate with everybody, and there are a whole lot of Muslims in this world to do business with. And they need guns so they can keep killing each other. Shiites and Sunnis and what not. And we'll sell them the guns.

He then pulls up his chair and sits facing Melania.

Donald — (softly) But see... I can talk to you like that... but to my base... I need to give them easy targets for their frustrations. I know that what we have in place is keeping us pretty safe... but how can you beat the kind of press we've been getting on the travel ban? The minute I announce it, all these crazy liberals storm out of their nooks and crannies, waving signs and banners. And my people were dumbfounded. They said to themselves, 'we can't believe there's so many immigrant lovers in our country.' And those are the folks that come to my rallies and got me elected. Of course, I could've said to them, listen up, globalization is here to stay, so buck up and get ready to understand multiculturalism... and a Muslim will soon be mayor of your city. But we wouldn't be here in the White House, would we?

She sits back.

Donald — The good news is that eventually, and this is my promise to you, after the folks in my base—the rich and the poor—have benefitted from my tax cuts and from deregulation and have their tummies full and are perhaps beginning to choke from the rise in greenhouse emissions and we don't have immigrants to do the dirty jobs... then I go back to them and say, 'hey, folks, we need to change direction'.
Melania — Shameless is not the word...
Donald — Look, let me go a step further. Don't think for a minute, that I'm fooling anybody. My people are smart folks. Very smart. They know that the world is getting smaller, that mixing it up and multiculturalism is inevitable. All they're saying is they don't want to go through the pain of adaptation right this moment. Let the next generation do it. And I came along and provided a rationale...
Melania — A mirage is what you offered.
Donald — ... And they said, 'let's go with the huckster from New York'.

She stands up and goes to the window.

Melania — What if I went out and told the world all what you just told me?

He gets up and crosses to be at her side.

Donald — You wouldn't do it.
Melania — Why not?
Donald — Because you're a decent human being and you love me. I wouldn't've married you otherwise. Besides...
Melania — What?
Donald — You've known all along what I am.

She is silent.

Donald — And you stayed.
Melania — Yes.

They pause.

Donald — Look... we can still have a good time... if we stop being so damn moral about it.
Melania — Easy to say.
Donald — The protestations of the left will soon fade... they'll get tired... seeing that my base is not budging... and since the Russia thing has got nothing to do with me... it'll be smooth sailing for the next 4 years, give or take a few. Then I'll decide if I want to run again. If it's any consolation... you can look at it this way... the nation is greater than the President they elect.
Melania — There's a lot of harm you can do.
Donald — And a lot of good.

He turns to look at her.

Donald — You look cute in that scarf.
Melania — Thank you.
Donald — I promise you, I will work on building bridges... but first I need to put some money in people's pockets. Happy people are more willing to build bridges.

Now she turns to look at him.

Melania — I'm adopting an orphan Muslim child from Africa... from one of the countries you want to suspend travel from.

He narrows his eyes.

Donald — I see. From a slum in Yemen... Sudan... Somalia... directly to the White House. Doesn't it seem a bit extreme?
Melania — Not at all... and it would do wonders for your presidency.
Donald — Don't do anything for my presidency, please. If you go ahead with that madness... we'll likely be accused of blatant, shameful manipulation of public opinion.

Melania — I don't care what they say. I want the child to be a little girl.

Donald — You had talked about having another child... so it would be born here, in the White House. Don't you want to do that instead?

Melania — I've decided not to be pregnant again. I want to explore my mind instead.

Donald — You're moving along on that front.

Melania — Thank you. And afterwards... I'd like to get her a little sister... from Central America. See, I read the budget. I know you've decided to cut foreign aid. But I'm an immigrant and I know this country to be compassionate... and if you don't want to behave as such... then it falls to me to do so... because that is who we are.

His phone rings. He takes it out of his coat pocket to answer.

Donald — Yes, Reince? (pause) I'll be over in a minute. (turning to her again) Reince telling me about another bombing in Afghanistan. Looks like we're never going to get out of there. Where were we?

Melania — The adoption.

Donald — Oh yes. By the way, you know how much money we've spent in Afghanistan since 2002? I asked and they said they'd get back to me with a precise figure, but he said it was in the order of billions and billions... like the stars in the universe. And I said, a trillion? And he said, "We're getting close".

Melania — How much of that has gone into building bridges?

Donald — (he chuckles) I've no idea.

Melania — That's what the adoption is about.

He gets up.

Donald — I need to get back. We'll think about all this. I'll see you tonight.

He rises and heads for the door. He turns...

Donald — Please take that scarf off.

And he exits.

She gets up and crosses to the mirror. She looks at herself.

Melania — Do I really think I can impact the world and not be laughed off as some nut?
Am I really doing this for him or to bring attention to myself?
(she slowly takes her scarf off)
Can I keep loving him with all his flaws...?
Am I willing to confront my own?
Do I leave?

3/29/17 — Trump tweets—If the people of our great
country could only see how viciously and inac-
curately my administration is covered by certain
media!

3/29 — He tweets—@FLOTUS Melania and I were honored
to stop by the Women's Empowerment Panel this
afternoon at the @WhiteHouse.

3/30 — He tweets—The Freedom Caucus will hurt the
entire Republican agenda if they don't get on the
team, & fast. We must fight them, & Dems, in 2018!

3/30 — He tweets—The meeting next week with
China will be a very difficult one in that we can
no longer have massive deficits… and job losses.
American companies must be prepared to look at
other alternatives.

3/30 — He tweets—Only by enlisting the full poten-
tial of women in our society will we be truly able
to #MakeAmericaGreatAgain.

14

It's mid afternoon and the sun shines through the open window. Melania is sitting nearby, in front of an easel with a sheet of canvas stretched out on it. The canvas is blank. On a small side table lies a palette, brushes and tubes of paint. On her lap she holds a sketch pad where she is drawing with a pencil.

Melania — I'm discovering that I like politics. I don't think I'd ever want to run for office. I think I'm quite clear about that. But I'd like to help set up a political party... a Women's Party... or... an immigrant party... Immigrants for America Party. I like the sound of that. It would help sharpen the debate about the contributions immigrants make. I'll keep it to myself for now. For the big elections, we'll fall in with the party that is open to a dialogue. I wonder how many signatures would be needed to get that going? Once I get back to New York, I'll have someone look into it.
(she gets up and stands in front of the window)
Would it be too polarizing? Maybe. But we need to come together to make our case. And at our meetings people would tell their stories, and those who are getting ahead would help guide those just getting started. Rich and poor, black and white... Islamic and Christian. And it would help us become better citizens. Better Americans. From the get go. The day will come when the world will become one people.

She returns to sit before her canvas and to continue drawing on her sketch pad.

Now Donald opens the door and steps in.

Melania — Hey. What are you doing here?
Donald — Taking a quick break. No major crises in the world at this time.

Pointing to the painting set-up which he is seeing for the first time.

Donald — What is this?

Melania — Surprise!

Donald — I didn't know you wanted to paint?

Melania — I've always wanted to try, just never got around to it. But now that we're here, with so many works of art around us, I'm inspired.

Donald — I thought you were going to a school to read to the children?

Melania — I did that already.

Donald — How did it go?

Melania — Very well. One of the children asked me if you knew when his parents would be coming back.

He is speechless.

Melania — He was born here but his parents came from Mexico and didn't have papers.

Donald — What kind of school did you go to?

Melania — A regular American school... with children whose parents come from all over the world.

Donald — I'm sorry, baby, but we'll have to better select where you do your readings.

Melania — Oh no. That is my business, and I won't have you interfering with it. What do you want me to do, choose a private school with children of wealthy parents?

Donald — God dammit! I'm taking a break and I have to get into a policy discussion with you. I'm fed up with this!

Melania — Why are you so upset? The issue is tearing up the nation, why can't we have a rational discussion about it?

Donald — Because I'm taking a break!

He turns around and heads for the door.

Melania — I gave him the number to the White House and asked him to give you a call. Surely you could explain better than me.

Donald — (stopping, turning back, speaking calmly) You couldn't just tell him that his parents were breaking the law, and that Donald Trump is putting an end to illegal immigration, once and for all?

Melania — I suppose I could have. Instead I asked him to come close and sit next to me. And I asked him what his parents did for a living. And he said his father did construction and his mother cleaned houses.

Donald — And you did that in front of the rest of the kids?

Melania — I did.

Donald — You couldn't just tell him that his parents were taking jobs from people born in this country? Or you just didn't think he would understand that?

Melania — I could have... but maybe those jobs couldn't be filled...

Donald — But they would have if the wages had been higher...

Melania — And maybe there was a pressing need and that was all that could be paid... and if no Americans showed up then the job wouldn't've got done...

Donald — Are you in favor of illegal immigration?

Melania — Of course not. But there has to be a better way to solve this problem than the way you're going about it. There has to be a better way than to stoke people's fears without thinking of the consequences. What about holding a national referendum on immigration?

Donald — The election *was* a referendum.

Melania — If so, you lost the popular vote by nearly three million.

Donald — (he takes a breath, looks her in the eye and smiles) I was tired of building hotels.

Melania — The child will be calling.

He says nothing for a moment. Then he picks up a chair from the table and carries it over so he can sit opposite her by the easel.

Donald — Can't you just love me the way I am?

Melania — I love you, Dee... I'm just not accepting you.

Donald — Why do I get the sense that you're slipping away from me...?

Melania — There are sides of us that have surfaced... and we've had a rough time looking at them.

Donald — They're pulling us apart. Do you want that?

Melania — I don't. I have been trying...

Donald — I know I've been... uncouth... impulsive... prejudiced... and yes, atavistic and totemic, to use those blessed words of yours... but do you believe that underneath all of it, I want to do well?

Melania — By whose standards?

Donald — My own, of course.

Melania — That's not good enough. The standards you've lived by when you were in real estate were one thing... the standards you need to live by now that you're President, are a whole different thing. And you have not made the switch... nor do you seem to want to, as you made clear to me the other day. If, God forbid, there was another terrorist attack in our land, you would go right back to beating your drum and demonizing Muslims. You would not try to find perspective.

Donald — Melania... I haven't been in office ten weeks... I need time. We need time.

Melania — You really want me by your side?

Donald — Yes, I do. Very much.

Melania — The way you talked the other day was so detached... so callous... so self-serving... I don't know that I can live with you that way.

She reaches over and takes his hand in hers.

Melania — (with sadness) We've had a good life, Dee... I wouldn't change it for anything...

Donald — C'mon, Melania... don't leave now... I know I'm a work in progress... I came to the presidency unprepared... and so did you. We can look at this as a new beginning. I just want you to be patient with me.

He takes her hand to his lips and kisses it.

Melania — You think you'll be able to stand up to the rich in your base, so you can help the poor?

Donald — I don't know... I really don't. But maybe I can evolve to that position... maybe I can... maybe it's in me.

Melania — I need to see you really trying, Dee. I know you love being in the limelight... but this is so different from the hotels... this job comes with harsh scrutiny of your intellect... you're the leader of the Free World... but you're settling for angry outbursts and tweeting. That won't do. You're not fooling anyone.

Donald — Myself, maybe.

Melania — The protestations of the left will not fade... they won't because you're not growing up politically and it is so clear. Keep this up and you will fail.

He lowers his head for a moment.

Donald — What do you think I should do?

Melania — You were once a democrat.

Donald — I was.

Melania — Reach over. Make alliances.

Donald — The party won't forgive me.

Melania — First you must learn to govern.

She gets up and taking him by the hand crosses to the window. They stand next to each other, facing out.

Melania — You were elected to the office to solve problems... to bring out the best in everyone... so we can pull together and move forward. It will take bipartisanship to do that... and less inequality... and less violence.

He puts his arm around her shoulders.

Donald — It's not like I couldn't live without you... we've been there before... it's just that... together we're better... more so now that you've had the courage to emerge and be vocal.

Melania — I didn't think you liked it...

Donald — I didn't... but I don't always know what's good for me.

They smile at each other.

Donald — And that idea you had about starting a department of Motivation and Race Relations—MORR... come to think of it, it comes awfully close to moor, as in the Arab conquerors of Spain, doesn't it?
Melania — It does.

They chuckle.

Melania — No irony there.
Donald — I don't think that idea is crazy at all. But I'll need to work on it. Or we both will... and find the right time and place for it.
Melania — We have a lot of work ahead.
Donald — We do.

15

April 3rd 2017 — 11:00 pm. Melania is in bed reading the newspaper. Donald steps out of the bathroom in his robe and sits at the table.

At that very moment, at 6 am on April 4th, 7 hours ahead and nearly 5900 miles east—from an air base in Syria, Bashar al Assad's planes have taken off to launch an attack on the town of Khan Shaykhun, in the northern province of Idlib, a town held by forces opposed to his regime.

Donald — I'm not sleepy. Must be that diet you put me on.
Melania — I'll give you a massage, it'll relax you.
Donald — Thank you, baby.
Melania — You're welcome.

She puts down the newspaper, gets up and crosses to stand behind him, and she starts to massage his neck and shoulders.

Donald — You know that's one of your secret weapons, don't you?
Melania — Not so secret anymore.
Donald — Ahh... that feels good. You still want to adopt the children?
Melania — Yes.
Donald — Can you wait on that?
Melania — Why?
Donald — I know you won't have any trouble adopting on your own... but wouldn't it be better if we both did it?
Melania — It would.
Donald — I just need a little time.
Melania — How long?
Donald — Till the end of summer?
Melania — Do you really want to do it?

Donald — I still think it would hurt my presidency.

Melania — It would be sending a strong signal to the world... a radical departure from the way you've conducted yourself so far.

Donald — It would give us more time to think about it.

Melania — I've made my choice. But I can wait for you.

Donald — How do you think my base will react?

Melania — I'd like to think you'll touch their hearts but I don't know.

Donald — They won't drop me?

Melania — I don't think so. But I don't want to mislead you. It's your presidency. I'm just the first lady.

Donald — Let's go for a walk.

Melania — Now?

Donald — Yes, now. That touch of yours is giving me energy instead.

Melania — Let me put something on.

Minutes later they're strolling on the White House lawn. It's a beautiful night, the stars above shining brightly.

Donald — You know what else I haven't got credit for?

Melania — What's that?

Donald — Defeating the House of Clinton and the House of Bush.

Melania — (laughs) Sounds monarchical.

Donald — Not just defeating them, but putting them out of business. If Hillary had got elected she would've been in there for 8 years. By then the party would've groomed Chelsea to take over. And the same with Jeb. After his 8 years then it would've been his son. But I knocked them out. All of them. I'm pretty proud of that. The American people owes me.

Melania — To hear you talk, it seems you have in mind ushering in the House of Trump.

Donald — Very good, Melania. And it doesn't take a genius to see the family together and realize that we're made of a very special stock.

Melania — I much prefer a Republic than anything connected to succession.

Donald — But wait. I'm quite aware of the importance for the nation of finally having a woman president.

Melania — (looking at him) Ivanka?

Donald — Bingo. And what better preparation for the job than to be in on all policy decisions for 8 consecutive years. Meeting world leaders, dealing with crises, being there for the ups and the downs. She'd know everybody on the world stage, be on a first name basis with anyone worth mentioning.

Melania — It's not about knowing people... you need to have a vision...

Donald — As soon as she gets comfy in her job of Special Adviser, I'll start sending her out as special envoy to do this or that for me. And I'd start with China.

Melania — They love her over there.

Donald — Exactly. That would give her a taste of all the goodies to come.

Melania — But don't you think Mike would want to run against her?

Donald — Sure. And so would a thousand other people. But by then the nation would have a clear understanding that a Trump is a Trump. And there would be so many achievements to point to that there would be no contest. But now that you mention it, if I ever get the sense that Mike is starting to think of himself as presidential material, why then, for the next election, I'll get myself a different VP.

Melania — You would do that?

Donald — Sweetheart, politics is a blood sport and Mike knows it. Besides, I put him there.

Melania — Ivanka might want to put Jared in as her running mate.

Donald — That wouldn't be cool. I like him, don't get me wrong, but if he gets in, then he would want to start the House of Kushner and that's not the same. Being the First Gentleman of the nation is a pretty high honor. That should be sufficient.

Melania — A Trump dynasty...

Donald — Why not?

Melania — And in my view, antidemocratic.

Donald — Of course, it would be up to the voters. The thing that Ivanka would have over everybody else is that by the time she runs, her trust, from all the money her brand would have made, would be worth billions and billions. And billionaires don't lose elections.

Melania — You're forgetting Ross Perot.

Donald — Perot?

Melania — Remember, third party candidate from Texas?

Donald — He didn't have the charm.

Melania — Oh but he did.

Donald — There's always an exception to the rule. Billionaires should not lose elections, not just because of the money itself, but because of what the money says about you. That you have passion, that you have brains, that you have problem solving ability, stamina, etc. Need I go on?

Melania — I've been thinking about starting a new political party...

He stops.

Donald — This is the second time you mention it.

Melania — A Women's Party.

Donald — You're not serious?

Melania — Women need to have a stronger political voice. Look at your cabinet, 5 women out of 33 members. We cannot wait. We have to stand up now.

Donald — I can assure you that in 8 years, Ivanka will be more than ready.

Melania — If she really wants it, let her compete with everybody else. Besides, we don't have 8 years.

Donald — A women's party will end up polarizing the nation.

Melania — Any more so than it is now?

Donald — That's going to get resolved.

Melania — When? Building bridges is not your forte.

Donald — I thought you were going to help me with that?

Melania — I am. If you let me.

Donald — If you think that women are going to flock to a women's party, thinking that it would be liberating, you're wrong. The women who voted for me weren't oppressed, they wanted their

154

husbands to get better jobs so they could stay home and be the housewife. You need to do your research.

Melania — I will.

Donald — If you start a women's party, come the next election, they will want to field a candidate against me.

Melania — If you evolve and become a President to all Americans, then you would have nothing to fear, would you?

Donald — Who would you vote for?

Melania — I would vote for the best candidate.

Donald — And you would do so with a clear conscience?

Melania — Yes.

They look into each other's eyes.

Melania — Because the Republic is as important as my love for you.

A frantic call rings out from near the White House. It's the Chief of Staff racing across the lawn towards them.

Reince — Mr. President! Mr. President!

Reince catches up to them, panting from the run, a look of alarm.

Donald — Reince, what're you doing here so late?

Reince — I had some work to do. I called you but you didn't answer.

Donald — I left my phone inside. What's going on?

Reince — Jim just called, from Defense. Assad launched a chemical weapons attack. Gassed his own people. The pictures we're getting, they're horrible... the kids...

He takes her aside.

Donald — I have to go.

She holds his face in her hands and kisses him.

Melania — I love you.
Donald — Love you, too. Don't do the women's party, please.

While facing her still, he steps back to join Reince, then they pivot and begin to make their way towards the White House. She looks after him.

They walk a stretch, then he turns back for one last look at her.

Melania — (locking eyes she calls out) Love...

He smiles as he waves goodbye.

Melania — (and she calls out again) I said love...

And he blows her a final kiss.

Donald — Is a many splendored thing.

The End

AFTERWORD

In the attack on Khan Shaykhun, the toxic gas Sarin was released, killing 74 people and injuring 557 according to local authorities. The Assad regime denied the charges.

Three days later, on April 7th, the United States fired off 59 cruise missiles against the Shayrat Air Base in Syria, from where the chemical attack had been launched.

As of July 27th 2017, the republican party has repeatedly failed to repeal or replace Obamacare.

ACKNOWLEDGMENT

My special thanks to Coco for her support and
suggestions. And to Ann Altmark for reading
the manuscript and her words of encouragement.

My gratitude to American journalists, for their
indefatigable courage and unbending commitment
to the free exchange of ideas.

www.ingramcontent.com/pod-product-compliance
Lightning Source LLC
Chambersburg PA
CBHW030651110726
47901CB00002B/670